Stories in These United States

Stories in These United States

FOR YOUNG AND OLD

Margery Dorian

VANTAGE PRESS
New York

Published by Vantage Press, Inc.
516 West 34th Street, New York, New York 10001

Manufactured in the United States of America
ISBN: 0-533-10269-3

Library of Congress Catalog Card No.: 92-90738

0 9 8 7 6 5 4 3 2 1

To my mother and father

Contents

Stories in These
United States

Helena's Search:
An Early California Tale

Horse Thieves

It was a late June evening and the shadows were deepening. A *carreta* with its heavy oaken wheels bumped along, its driver whipping the two oxen. He was trying to cover mileage before nightfall. The two occupants of the *carreta* were huddled together.

"Helena, whatever happens," a young woman's voice spoke in Spanish, "promise me you will always keep the golden locket your father gave you. Some day you will show it to my California family in Monterey."

Helena whispered in her mother's ear, "Yes, Mother, I will always treasure the picture of my father. I am proud to wear jewelry that came from the court of Russia. The locket is safely hidden under my bodice."

She pressed against her mother's warmer body as the *carreta* bounced across the deep ruts of a dusty and stony roadway.

Already Helena was sore from being thrown about. The *carreta* had left the Bodego Bay rancho early that morning, its destination the settlement of Sonoma. It was carrying goods to the Sonoma rancho of General Mariano Vallejo: elegant dress material delivered to Bodego Bay by a French schooner and, more important, bundles of otter furs once stored at Fort Ross, now abandoned by its Russian settlers.

Helena was curious. "Why did my father take us to the rancho at Bodego Bay?"

"Your father, Helena, worked for the Russian-American Fur Company. He took the furs with us to the rancho that became our new home, but he died before the furs were sold."

Behind the *carreta* were roped two handsome stallions for the general. The oxen managed the level turf with some ease, but when there was a small rise, the driver struck the two animals a resounding blow.

Helena cringed.

"Put your head on my lap," said her mother. "Tonight you can slumber on that straw mat in back. We will have to keep each other warm."

"It is a night for coyotes," said the driver. "Always when the moon is full."

Helena listened. She could hear the howl of a wild animal, perhaps a wolf, perhaps a coyote.

"There's another sound," continued the driver.

Yes, in the distance sounded the regular beat of horses' hoofs. The horses attached to the *carreta* started to neigh.

The driver, a rough fellow, spoke reassuringly, although he seemed perturbed. "Don't know why you made this trip with the likes of me . . . too dangerous for a lady and her pretty daughter."

The driver stopped the *carreta*. Helena could hear the continuous clatter of horses' hoofs and the cries of approaching riders. She cuddled close to her mother as the roar and cries of the night riders pierced the cold night air. The driver seemed half-paralyzed when a pack of horses, Indians mounted on their saddleless backs, charged into view.

All that Helena remembered was a shot from a rifle. She grabbed her mother's skirt as the body of the driver plunged to the ground. In the half-darkness, she saw a band of Indians descend on the *carreta*. One of the tribe, the leader no doubt, cut the horses loose from the cart and tied each to two of their stallions. The tribe was not

4

interested in the contents of the cart, nor in the mother trembling with fright, her daughter clinging to her.

In a few minutes, the Indians were off in the night. The coyotes struck up another chorus of howls.

But what of the driver knocked to the ground by a rifle shot, his stomach torn open by the jab of a tomahawk? Terrified, Senora Avila climbed out of the *carreta* and tried to pull the tomahawk from the wound.

But she could see that the poor man was dead. Wiping the blood on her skirt, she climbed back in the *carreta* beside Helena. Somehow the ordeal had brought her new strength. She took Helena's hand and whispered, "Without the two horses in the rear, it will be easier to drive the oxen. We will continue to move towards Sonoma."

It was fortunate there was a full moon. Before taking the reins in hand, Senora Avila located the feed bag for the oxen under the driver's seat. Stalwart animals, they still needed to have sustenance to continue on a roadway filled with holes and puddles from an overflow of water from a creek.

In the excitement, Helena had dropped the beloved Russian shawl on the ground. She picked it up and climbed back on the *carreta* seat next to her mother. There was no sound from the retreating Indians, only from the coyotes that bayed at the moon.

"I hope we can get to the Petaluma settlement soon after dawn," whispered Senora Avila. "I understand Sonoma is not too far from there. Helena, double the shawl around you. These California nights are so cold."

Helena was reassured, sitting close to her mother on the driver's seat. If only her dear father were with them! How she did miss him since that terrible day when he was mortally wounded by a wild bronco. In Russia, he had ridden only tame horses in the parks of St. Petersburg.

5

Here in California, as an envoy of the czar, he was not used to the rugged ranch life. Her mother and father had become acquainted in Monterey, her mother's home, when he came to the capital to trade furs with the Californians. It was impossible to sleep in the lumbering old *carreta*. Helena saw that her mother was becoming more and more exhausted. "Here, Helena, take the reins, dear. I do feel a little faint."

Helena did as told just in time, as her mother's body became limp. Helena pulled on the reins to stop the oxen, then rubbed her mother's forehead and chest. She did not know what else to do.

Prince Solano

Helena continued to drive the oxen.

"I'm glad I have you," said her mother.

Stillness! More stillness!

"Please sing," asked her mother. "Sing that lovely Russian song your father taught you—the one about the birds."

Helena's voice was as soft as honey, as melodious as a meadowlark. . . . When she finished, her mother asked her to sing a song in Spanish.

Presently they were startled by a horse bearing a giant of a man. The horse pulled up alongside the *carreta*. Helena could see that the rider had a most noble bearing. In the moonlight, she could discern a cavalier erect in his saddle, dressed in the clothes of a Californian gentleman, a low-crowned sombrero with a handkerchief tied over his forehead and under his chin. A poncho covered his shirt, and he carried a lasso around the horn of the saddle.

The cavalier rode a cream-colored horse with a silver-white mane, and he spoke in Spanish with a slight accent. Helena had to hold her oxen in check while his horse snorted and whinnied.

"*Buenas noches*," said the man. "Is this the proper way for two ladies to travel? I must say I enjoyed the senorita's singing."

Helena could see that here was someone to help them. She quickly told the gentleman the story of their travels from Bodego Bay and that they were headed for the Sonoma rancho of Don Mariano Vallejo.

"He is my friend," said the horseman. "He is a good man. He will be happy to welcome you when he returns from Monterey, and he will find lodging for you."

Senora Avila told how the horses were stolen and that their driver had been killed. The cavalier seemed angry. "I will see that these horse thieves are punished."

Helena wondered how he could know or guess who these thieves were.

"I am Prince Solano, and my best friend is the Comandante Vallejo."

How lucky she and her mother were, thought Helena.

Prince Solano continued. "I am an Indian belonging to the Suisun tribe. Unfortunately, we are not as powerful as we used to be."

"Do you think these thieves were part of your tribe?" asked Helena.

"*Si*, senorita, I know they were . . . and I shall see that they are punished."

"They were cruel to shoot our driver," said Helena. "Pardon me, senor. How is it you are a prince?"

"It is a long story, senorita, which I will tell you some day. But let me say that I am Chief Sem Yeto of the Suisun tribe, but I was baptized into the Christian religion and am called by some Prince Solano. None other of my tribe has been baptized."

"I am glad to be acquainted with a prince," said Helena.

"Let us proceed. You, young lady, can ride on my horse Presto. I will try to make your mother comfortable in the wagon."

He took his poncho and covered Senora Avila's shoulders. Afterwards he helped Helena onto the back of his stallion. Helena accepted the reins, happy someone had come to rescue them.

8

Prince Solano climbed into the wagon next to Helena's mother. "Presto knows the road," he said to Helena. Seeing that she was frightened, he added, "He will lead us to Petaluma and then on to Sonoma."

The caravan continued in near darkness although the moon was helping to light the way. Dawn broke as the horse and wagon ploughed forward. It was not until late morning that they reached the sprawling settlement of Petaluma. After tortillas at the home of Prince Solano's friends, they were refreshed enough to make their final trek to Sonoma.

"I will take you to my good friend's home; he lives near Don Vallejo," said the prince. "The Gonzales family will be happy to welcome you."

It was almost nightfall before Prince Solano escorted his two tired companions to the *casa* of Senor and Senora Gonzales.

Pedro Gonzales

Helena awakened to the barking of a dog. Where was she?

"That's our sheepdog, Cano," said a small boy as he peeked through a grilled window. "My name is Pedro. I am ten years old."

The boy disappeared as Helena turned. She could hear her mother groaning from other side of the room. Poor Mother! She did not know they were both safe in the home of Prince Solano's friends.

The sun was streaming through the window protected with heavy iron bars. Helena was remembering what had happened when Prince Solano had escorted them to this friendly home. How secure she felt in the *casa* of Senora Gonzales! How good the touch of those warm, woolen blankets felt during the night!

The buxom figure of Senora Gonzales marched through the doorway with two cups of steaming hot chocolate.

"*Gracias*," said Helena. "*Muchas gracias!*"

Her mother stirred and lifted her head from her mat on the floor. "I am sorry we are making you so much trouble," she managed to say in her weak voice.

"Senora, it is no trouble. . . . We want you to feel well. We will send by post for Dr. Marsh. When he comes he will make you well. For breakfast we will bring you some tortillas."

"*Mas tarde*," said Senora Avila. "Helena can help you prepare them."

"*Otra vez* . . . another time," said Senora Gonzales.

10

Pedro put his head to the grilled window again. "I want to show the senorita the *casa* of the comandante."

After Helena dressed, she went out to the courtyard. Pedro was waiting for her. "This is my sheepdog, Cano," said Pedro. His dark eyes were as soulful as the dog's.

"He likes you," offered Pedro. "He doesn't like everyone."

"Is that big house over there . . . does that belong to the Comandante Vallejo?" asked Helena.

"It's an adobe house, but three times bigger than ours," offered Pedro. "Don Vallejo is very rich. He owns thousands of cattle and is in charge of all the land grants. . . ."

"What does that mean?" asked Helena.

"He just gives land to anybody who wants it, I guess," said Pedro. "I think maybe you would like to know some of the comandante's children."

"First, I want to know if Prince Solano found our horses the Indians stole," said Helena.

"Yes, he brought them here to the rancho for Don Vallejo. He was going to punish the Indians, but they were sick—had smallpox all over them. Many of the Suisun Indians have died because they were not vaccinated in time."

"Have you been vaccinated?" asked Helena.

"Oh, yes. . . . We do not wish to have smallpox. Someone is coming from the Mission San Rafael to finish giving the vaccinations. You must have it done."

Helena felt she must go inside to see how her mother was. Senora Gonzales was standing a few feet from her guest. "Right now, I want my guest to be comfortable. Perhaps she needs another blanket."

Senora Avila spoke haltingly. "I am so hot . . . my back hurts. . . . I do not know why I feel so sick."

Helena started to take her mother's hand, but Senora Gonzales stopped her. She whispered, "Do not take your mother's hand until after you are vaccinated."

Poor Senora Avila! Poor Helena! She was overcome with anxiety.

"We will let your mother sleep until we have medical help from the mission."

Pedro was looking through the doorway. "Come with me and Cano," he said. "I will show you more of the rancho and the barracks, though now there are no soldiers there. You can ride one of the broncos, that is, if you are not afraid."

"I hate horses," said Helena. "My father was killed breaking a bronco."

Music in the Vallejo Casa

Helena left her mother in the care of Senora Gonzales. She found Pedro in the patio leaning against a post. He was gazing at a hummingbird nested in the red peppers and water ollas.

"Perhaps you would like to see the new piano of the comandante. It was shipped around the cape from the United States," said Pedro, trying to divert Helena's attention from her sick mother.

"I have only seen one piano in my life," said Helena. "Governor Rotchef brought one from Sitka, Alaska, to Fort Ross for his wife, Helena. She was a favorite in the court in Russia. At least, this is what my father told me."

"Are you named for the wife?" asked Pedro.

"Yes, in a way. Princess Helena Rotchef was my godmother and then later the mountain in our valley was called Mount Helena. I don't know if I'm named for a mountain or a princess."

"It really doesn't make any difference," said Pedro. "Anyhow, I would like to show you the piano here at the rancho of the Vallejos. Don Vallejo gave me the permission to enter the parlor in the mornings. I cannot play, but all his children are studying. I heard you singing to your mother last night, and it was very good."

Pedro and Helena refrained from talking as they walked toward the big adobe *casa* with its gardened terrace. Sounds of piano playing came from the open windows.

"The children of Don Vallejo have their lessons every

13

day with Herr Hoeffner. He came all the way to California from Germany. He is very strict," explained Pedro.

Helena listened to a piece some child was playing. She did not recognize it. "I wish I could play," she said.

"You sing very well," encouraged Pedro. "Maybe Herr Hoeffner would take you for a pupil."

The children waited for the piano lesson to finish. Then Pedro led Helena from the patio into the parlor. In the corner stood a shiny square piano.

"*Buenas dias*," Herr Hoeffner greeted them with a rather strange accent.

Pedro took courage. "My friend here, she has a good voice. She sings like a bird."

"That is interesting, Pedro. Perhaps she will sing for my piano students and me."

Helena did not have to be asked a second time. She burst into one of her favorite songs, "La Paloma."

Herr Hoeffner did not applaud when she finished, but he looked pleased.

"Helena's father was Russian," offered Pedro. "She tells me she sings Russian songs."

"Some other time," said Herr Hoeffner. "Andronico is playing a piece by the famous composer Schumann. Epifania has an easier piece by Mozart composed when he was a little boy."

Helena decided Epifania was about her age. "May I listen?" she asked.

"*Natürlich*, senorita."

Helena and Pedro sat on a wooden bench while the two Vallejo children took turns playing for their small audience.

Senora Gonzales appeared at the doorway. "Helena, you must come quickly. Your mother is very sick and calls for you."

14

Helena dashed off for the Gonzales *casa*, racing over the turf to the guest room of the Gonzales house.

"Mama, Mama," she cried. "Do not be sick. . . . I cannot be here alone."

A man in uniform stopped her from reaching her mother. "Your mother is very ill . . . probably has smallpox," said the officer. "I have come to vaccinate those who have not been treated. I am sure you are one of these. It is important not to have contact with anyone afflicted with the disease."

"I want to die," wailed Helena.

Senora Avila turned her head toward her daughter. "Helena, you must go to Monterey, to my family there. I am afraid I will not be able to go with you. . . . I hope you are wearing your golden locket."

Her energy was spent and she said no more. The officer tried to vaccinate Helena, who was pacing around the room like a wounded animal. . . . He finally did.

Pedro was standing outside in the courtyard. He wanted to show his sympathy for a little girl who had lost her father and now her poor mother.

Senora Gonzales came out and took Helena's hand. "You will stay with us as long as you wish," she said.

The Flag of the Republic of California

A month passed and only now was Helena able to smile. Her mother could not combat the disease and had died, unable to hold her child in her arms. Father Altamira from the Sonoma mission had performed the last rites and prayed for Helena to have the strength to live again.

Senora Gonzales treated Helena as her own child. Helena helped with the meals. She ground the grain on the stone *metete*, then added water to the flour. She did not go to the Vallejo *casa* with Pedro, as she did not feel like hearing music.

"Some day you will sing again," Pedro sympathized. "Your mother would want you to be happy. She was a lovely lady."

It was hard to be consoled. How could she have the courage to leave these wonderful friends, especially Pedro? But her mother had said she must travel to Monterey to be with her family. How would she ever manage to do this?

Senora Gonzales tried to divert Helena's thinking to some pleasant tasks. She asked Helena and Pedro to help a certain gentleman by the name of William Todd to assemble and design a new flag for the Republic of California. There was no more Mexican territory, only California, which was to be a free land, able to make its own decisions. In the upper left-hand corner of the flag, Helena placed a five-pointed star, and facing the star, Pedro placed a brown bear. Mr. Todd worked on the lettering, which said:

THE REPUBLIC OF CALIFORNIA

The flag was raised on the Plaza of Sonoma. Helena did not understand the meaning of the flag. She did not know that trouble was fermenting all over California, that the Comandante Vallejo was a true Mexican who realized California could no longer be controlled by Mexico or survive by itself. It was only the United States that had the energy to pull together all the factions that had been tearing at one another.

Helena and Pedro looked up at the new flag they had helped assemble. They wished that the comandante would return from Monterey and Yerba Buena. Perhaps he would put them all at ease.

Doña Vallejo was planning a fiesta to celebrate the return of her husband from his many duties. He was always traveling: Sacramento, Monterey, San Diego. Uprisings, conspiracies, and dissatisfaction with changes of governors were playing havoc with his good intentions.

The preparations for the fiesta were endless. There were the guests to be invited: friends, neighbors, militia. Neighbors could be notified by word of mouth, but those who lived at a distance would have a written invitation printed on a machine ordered from Mexico.

Of course there was the food to be cooked and served, the music and a dancing master to call the quadrilles. Old Tomo, the Indian who had survived the smallpox, could tell some Indian tales and, of course, Helena would sing. Doña Vallejo was delighted with the ideas.

Now that the date was set, it was imperative that Don Vallejo be there, as he was the host and the guest of honor.

The Fiesta for the Comandante

The preparations for the fiesta were well under way. Even Cano, the sheepdog, sensed that something important was going to happen.

"When will the comandante be here?" asked Helena. She was eager to see this great man who wrote poetry even though he was a military commander of soldiers.

"Don Vallejo was secretary to Governor Arguella," explained Pedro. "He will come here with his bodyguard in hopes of drilling the few remaining soldiers on the plaza. However, they have all left to quell the revolts of the Indian *vaqueros*."

Helena said wistfully, "I wish I could go to Monterey with the comandante. He is so generous. I saw a basket of gold coins for his guests in the parlor when I was singing my Russian song for the music professor."

"The comandante doesn't want anyone to be hungry or go away without plenty of money in their possession. He has been very generous with the land grants. Since he is director of colonization, he can give away as much land as he wants," said Pedro.

"He is truly a gentleman," said Helena.

Later that day, Helena and Pedro were seated in the patio of the Vallejo *casa* when a mounted courier descended from his horse and approached the children. "I have a message for Doña Vallejo from the comandante," said the courier.

"I will call her," offered Pedro. He ran through the open door into the parlor.

Helena could hear the strains of a military march the Vallejo children were preparing to play at the fiesta. In a few moments, Doña Vallejo appeared at the doorway. "Your message?" she queried.

"The comandante wishes to say he will be here for the ball on Thursday. He has been in Monterey with the governor but is anxious to see his family and all the guests."

Doña Vallejo was overjoyed. To the children, she said, "We shall hurry with the preparations. Prince Solano has promised to help with the horses and the stage coaches of the guests." She hurried into the *casa*.

"I wish I could go to Monterey with Don Vallejo," said Helena.

"Then I wouldn't see you any more," Pedro remarked.

"Perhaps your mother would let you go with me," Helena said in earnest.

"Who knows where the comandante will go next?" added Pedro.

Two more days to get ready. Helena was sewing on her frock, as she wanted to look her best for Don Vallejo. She put some extra tucks in the muslin sleeves of her plaid dress. She scalloped the ends of the sleeves, which she planned to draw up with bright red ribbons.

"What are you going to wear at the ball?" Helena asked Pedro.

"My mother says I have to wear my uniform. It has a lot of fancy stuff on the jacket. But I do like to wear the high-heeled boots and the cape."

"You will look very special," said Helena.

They both did look elegant at the ball. Don Vallejo stood at the doorway of the parlor to greet his guests. Helena thought he looked like the czar of Russia must have looked in Saint Petersburg. There was much gold braid and fancy buttons on the coat. The comandante was a handsome man and smiled at everyone.

Doña Vallejo stood next to her husband. Then came his brother, Salvador; his high-spirited and beautiful sister, Rosalia; and her husband, Jacob Leese. The military escort had been invited, but went on to the Petaluma settlement to be with their families.

"There must be a thousand people here," whispered Helena to Pedro.

"Not quite," said Pedro. "I counted them. There are about one hundred and sixty-eight."

It was time to enjoy the array of foods Doña Vallejo had ordered her servants to prepare. On a great hot bed of coals, a whole beef had been roasted; turkeys and chickens were tucked in at the sides. The guests retired to the patio to help themselves to tortillas, tamales, and enchiladas, heaped on large pewter platters.

Helena wasn't hungry. "I'm getting scared," she said. "I hope I shall remember all the Spanish words of my song. My mother said my Russian song, 'In the Meadow Stood a Birch Tree,' should be accompanied by a balalaika."

"I'm glad Doña Vallejo asked you to sing," said Pedro.

"Here comes the master of ceremonies."

"Epifania is going to play first. She's more scared than I am." Helena took Pedro's hand.

Epifania did play. Her brother managed to get lost, at least temporarily. Herr Hoeffner was angry and looked everywhere in the house for him.

"Never mind," said the comandante. "He's a real boy . . . wants to have a little fun."

Helena wished she could hide, too, but somehow she felt she should do her best for the guests. After Old Tomo had told some Indian stories, she sang several Spanish songs accompanied by two guitars. When it came to the Russian song, she explained the words to the guests. Everyone applauded. Encouraged, Helena broke into a *hopak* her father had taught her. Don and Doña Vallejo seemed pleased.

It was now time for the group dances: the contradances, the waltzes, and the jotas. A couple who came with the musicians performed a fandango with castanets. The man gathered the hats of the gentlemen guests and placed them one by one on his partner's head. Always dancing, she balanced them dexterously on her head as she continued her castanet playing.

Wine and beer were passed again and as the glasses clinked, the guests shouted, "Viva el comandante!" They wished to honor their host, a man they all admired.

Prince Solano, looking handsome in his Indian leather jacket heavy with beads and silver buttons, passed little cakes to the ladies. The servants were busy bringing more drinks and removing used glasses.

As the guitars continued to play, another servant rushed to the comandante, shouting, "Don Mariano, Don Mariano, there are men outside . . . dirty men. They do not speak Spanish. They ask for you . . . say they are here on orders from the Americans!"

The Arrest

The comandante followed the servant to the door. Helena could hear him say, *"Buenas tardes*, gentlemen . . . I see you have been traveling." Since he spoke in English, Helena could not understand. All she knew was that five or six disheveled and greasy-looking travelers were invited to join the party.

"We are happy to have you," said the comandante. "What brings you here?"

The tallest of the five spoke up. "We have come to arrest Comandante Vallejo. We have left our rifles outside."

"You have no need of them," said the comandante.

"We have orders from Captain Fremont to escort three of the Californians to Sacramento . . . you, Salvador Vallejo, and your secretary, Victor Prudon."

"But first, please enjoy our food and drink . . . we are happy to include you in our party," said Comandante Vallejo.

Helena wished she understood English. She saw the comandante serve the five men while the guests watched in amazement. Doña Vallejo, overcome with fear for her husband, collapsed on a chair. Prince Solano told her he would like to throw them all out.

Since there were no soldiers in the barracks at this time, the comandante ordered the keys to the door of the barracks where the munitions and equipment were stored. He turned over eight field pieces, two hundred stands of arms, and a hundredweight of powder to the intruders.

22

Knowing that Captain Fremont had ordered his arrest, Mariano Vallejo was not worried for his safety, but only for that of his wife and family. He bade goodnight to the guests and retired to his room to prepare for the journey to Sacramento.

Helena and Pedro walked home, both saddened by the unusual happenings. Prince Solano went with them. "Cano and I do not like these uninvited guests," he said. "In my mind, I shoot that big man. He follows orders of Captain Fremont. I know Don Vallejo believes California is better off as a state of the union. Texas has joined the union, so why not California?"

The evening had certainly taken an ugly turn. Helena was miserable. Such a nice man, Don Vallejo! How was she ever going to reach Monterey, now that the comandante was arrested?

Helena in Yerba Buena

Helena had hoped to travel to Monterey with Rosalia and Jacob Leese, who had a house there. But they decided to remain in Sonoma to help Doña Vallejo look after affairs.

Senora Leese said to her, "Helena, if you wish to remain here several months, you can travel with me to Monetery. But if you wish to go now, I suggest you take Cano for protection, embark on a launch from Port Novato, and sail directly to Yerba Buena. When you arrive in Yerba Buena, you can go with the dog directly to my husband's mercantile store. The manager there will see to it that you are a passenger on the mail cart to Monterey."

Helena was worried. "But how can I find my mother's family in Monterey?"

"Listen carefully . . . I shall write two letters, one to the manager of my husband's store in Yerba Buena and the other to your mother's family in Monterey. The second letter will ask your mother's family to meet the coach from Yerba Buena each day. That way, you will be able to find your relatives."

What a wonderful and beautiful lady!

The following week Helena said *adios* to the hospitable Gonzales family and the Vallejos, especially Rosalia Leese. There were Pedro and Prince Solano, her special friends. Helena patted the head of Cano, who was to be her companion on the next lap of her travels. Every day since the plan had been made, she was spending a lot of time with Cano. Her letter of identification was in her muslin traveling bag.

Time was drawing to a close. Helena was glad Don Vallejo had written from Sacramento that he was in good hands and that his family had nothing to fear. He was sure that Providence had guided the Americans to do the right thing. He promised he would be reunited with them soon.

It was early morning at Port Novato when Helena climbed into the small launch carrying mail and freight to Yerba Buena. "Yer m' only passenger," said the stalwart captain, who seemed happy to have some company aboard. Cano barked.

"And there's Cano, too," said Helena as she stroked the dog's back.

In a few minutes, the launch was pulling away from the dock. Helena fought back the tears as she waved to her good friends, Pedro and Senora Gonzales. In the morning fog, she could just see Prince Solano as he galloped over the high reeds of the estuary on his horse, Presto.

"Good-bye!" Helena shouted to all of them. "Please come and visit me!"

Now Helena was traveling all by herself. She checked to see if the letter from Senora Leese and a bone for Cano were in her muslin bag. Too frightened to cry, she stared ahead, but she could hardly see the captain through the fog.

"How's m' passenger?" yelled the captain, as he guided the craft from his crow's nest.

Cano barked. All was well as could be expected with no friends or family. Just one faithful dog!

Wisps of fog closed in on the little launch. In a way, it made Helena feel more secure. It was just a sea-faring home, bumping along with its noisy mechanical chatter.

Helena saw the captain was intent on his steering since it was so foggy, and she did not want to interrupt him with unimportant questions. Cano had already decided to take a nap since there was no cat to chase.

Helena looked at the piles of mailbags and wondered what all the letters said and to whom they were written. Hundreds of envelopes in each bag! She started to count the bags, but tired, she put her head down on Cano's soft, furry back.

Helena must have gone to sleep for a long time when she awoke with a start. It was the captain's voice shouting, "Yerba Buena . . . Yerba Buena . . . li'l gal . . . We're at the dock!"

The captain tried to help Helena as she rushed to get off the launch before the mail and the freight. Cano followed, sniffing at her heels. Once ashore, she looked down at her muslin bag and saw that it was open. With one hand she felt inside for the contents of the bag, and, to her horror, the letters with the important information and address of Mr. Leese's store were not there. Tearfully she looked at Cano; shreds of paper were sticking to his mouth.

"Oh, Cano, you have eaten the address of the store. What shall we do?"

Cano licked her hand. He looked so sorrowful.

"It doesn't do any good to be sorry, Cano." Helena was almost weeping. "What shall we do now?"

Why didn't she remember the whereabouts of the mercantile store of Jacob Leese? Since it was only the middle of the morning, she decided to walk through the busy streets of the downtown area. The fog had cleared and that made her feel better.

Helena passed a supply store for ships, an apothecary, and a trading post for seal and otter furs. As she was looking in the window and wondering what to do, an old woman, bedraggled and dirty, touched her shoulder. Helena pulled back.

"*Por favor*, I am hungry. Please give me some money," requested the woman.

Helena was saving a few coins, which she had been offered at the Vallejo house, but she put her hand in her sack and found the little purse.

"*Gracias, muchas gracias*," said the woman, and she disappeared in the crowd.

Before Helena had taken a few steps, a young boy with a fishing pole put his foot out in front of her to make her trip. She ignored the gesture and started to move on. "Where are you going?" asked the boy.

Helena ignored him again, but he followed her, one step behind.

"I see you give money. Who you looking for?" He was most persistent. Cano was biting at his heels.

"I want to go to the mercantile store of Mr. Leese," Helena confided.

The boy said he knew just where it was. He would take her there.

The Search Is Over

Helena followed the boy, who indicated the Leese store was around the corner.

"Just wait for me while I get rid of this fishing pole," he said, as he disappeared down an alley. He returned without the pole but with a rope. He looked at Cano, who was still growling.

"It is dangerous to walk through streets. I need tie rope to dog's collar. Someone steal him," said the boy.

Helena let the boy tie the rope on while Cano growled and started to bite him.

"Just wait here . . . " The boy grabbed the rope and pulled the dog along the cobblestone pavement against its will.

"Don't hurt my dog!" screamed Helena.

Before she could collect her wits, the dog and boy had disappeared behind a door. All she could hear were the muffled barks of Cano, who apparently didn't like his captor. She beat on the door and tried to open it, but it was locked from the inside.

What to do now? . . . She must find help. She ran helter skelter and soon seemed to have lost direction. People seemed too busy to pay any attention to her. Up one street, down another. Finally, she saw an old priest making his way toward her.

"Father," she cried to the priest. "Please help me."

The priest saw that Helena was in deep trouble. "What can I do for you, my dear child?"

"My dog has been stolen by a bad boy. He is behind a door and I do not know which door," said Helena.

"Of course you don't," said the priest in a consoling way.

Helena had at last found a friend. She told him her story and that she wanted to go to Monterey where her mother's family lived.

"I will take you to the mail wagon, which leaves about noon for Monterey. I am expecting to go there myself," said the priest.

"But what about Cano, my dog?" pleaded Helena.

"I will see that the commisionada makes a search for the dog. I expect from what you tell me that Cano will run away from this boy and find his way back to the home of the comandante in Sonoma."

"Do you really think so?" asked Helena.

"We must have faith in the Lord," said the priest.

Helena was so tired when she got on the mail wagon to Monterey that she almost forgot about Cano and fell asleep sitting between the driver and the kindly priest. For two days the mail cart rattled and twisted its way down El Camino Real to Santa Clara and over the Santa Cruz mountains.

When the horses were changed and the driver replaced at a station, she stretched her numb legs as she watched the activity, then climbed back to her place next to the priest. It was six o'clock on the second day of travel when the mail cart arrived at its destination of Monterey.

To Helena's surprise, she saw a family cart pull into the yard beside the mail cart. A woman jumped out and hurried to the mail cart. Helena did not need to ask who the lady was; she looked just like her mother. "It must be my aunt," shouted Helena to her friend.

The old priest smiled. "The Lord has provided," he said. "He will find your Cano, too."

The lady reached into the mail wagon and drew her sister's daughter to her. Helena could not help sobbing . . . She brushed her shoulder against that of her aunt.

"There is your uncle over there, waiting for you," said the lady. "He is taking your little bag to our wagon."

How good it was to have a family again. Helena's search was over. Tomorrow she would show her aunt and uncle the golden locket her father had given her. She did not know that the next day would be the day Commodore Sloat of the United States Navy would take down the flag of California on the Plaza of Monterey and replace it with the flag of the United States of America. Nor did she know that Comandante Vallejo was sadly burning the Mexican military uniforms that he would never wear again. It was July 7, 1846.

The Daytime Show

The Underground Spring

It was a warm morning in September 1849 when the babble of English and Spanish stopped abruptly. Young Helena of Sonoma had started to sing for the first time in English.

The ladies of the pueblo of Monterey were on their way to wash their clothes. Every week a caravan of *carretas* left their *casa* to travel to a hidden spring several miles from Monterey to do the wash.

Each family drove its oxen yoked to a wagon. Each *carreta* was full of soiled clothes. Some families brought teams of horses. Dirty linen covered the horses or oxen en route to the spring, and clean white linen was spread on their backs on the way home.

"Sing one more song," begged Senora O'Brien. Her *carreta* was behind Helena's Aunt Josefa's.

The laundry day was a festive occasion. The children went with their mother, as wash day was the day to picnic.

"I'll sing 'Camptown Races' again if everyone helps me with the chorus," announced Helena.

With the last la-la-la, Aunt Josefa's *carreta* came to a stop. The head *carreta* moved forward to give room to the other five wagons. They had arrived at the spring.

"Whoa there, *caballitos*," shouted Senora O'Brien to her horses. To Helena she called, "After we get settled and place our clothes in the spring, I want to talk to you. I do like your singing."

Helena helped Aunt Josefa dump the soiled clothes into the water holes. The tallow soap was rubbed into the rocks. Afterwards a great scrubbing took place. Helena loved the action. It made her want to sing again. She watched Senora O'Brien scrub her clothes and wondered what she had to tell her.

"After we have our picnic, I will talk to you," said Senora O'Brien.

Helena's three cousins were complaining to their mother. "I'm hungry, Mother," eight-year-old Maria said.

"How long do we have to wait for the picnic?" complained Dolores.

Carla said, "I hope Mother brought some tortillas. I'm starved."

Aunt Josefa listened patiently. "Helena may be just a bit older than you three girls . . . eleven, I believe. She knows how to work as well as sing."

"She's always singing around the house. Papa doesn't like it; he said so," said Dolores, who was a year younger than her cousin Helena and used to being the boss of her sisters.

After the washing had been completed, Aunt Josefa asked Helena to help wring out the water from the clothes and to spread each article on some nearby bush. It wasn't long before the whole family was seated on the dry earth or on a stone waiting to have the *merienda*, a picnic lunch.

Helena helped herself to a piece of chicken, a tortilla, and a persimmon. She took her food and climbed over to the other side of the water hole to sit next to Senora O'Brien.

"You are beginning to speak English very well," said Senora O'Brien. "When my husband taught you 'Camptown Races' and 'Old Black Joe,' he was pleased that you had such a good accent for English."

"Oh, thank you very much. I do want to sing American

34

songs as well as my Spanish and Russian ones," said Helena.

"My husband would like to teach you several more Stephen Foster songs."

"Really?" Helena said. Suddenly she looked downcast. "I wish my Uncle Luis would like my singing."

"You can always practice at our house," said Senora O'Brien. "What I did want to tell you is that Mr. Jack Swan is turning over part of his house to a group of actors. They are planning to make a small theatre there."

"A real live theatre?" asked Helena.

"Yes. Colonel Stevenson's recruits from New York are going to put on some minstrel shows. I understand the men sing and dance very well," said Senora O'Brien.

"Maybe I could sing some of my songs." Helena was almost breathless just thinking about this new venture.

"Of course, Patrick won't have much time to teach you this week, as he will be busy welcoming the delegates for the Constitutional Convention."

Helena and her cousins helped Aunt Josefa collect all the snow white laundry, which they folded and put in the *carreta*. Any clothes that were still damp they placed on the backs of the horses.

As the wheels of the *carreta* picked up dust on the way home, Helena sang to herself. She was happy to know there might be some place where she could present her songs.

Visiting the Theater

The next Saturday, Senor Patrick O'Brien called for Helena at Aunt Josefa's house. Uncle Luis was smoking his pipe by the wooden stove.

"Good day to you," said Patrick O'Brien to Uncle Luis. "I've come to kidnap that niece of yours. I want to introduce her to Jack Swan's new theater."

"I don't want her to get mixed up with a lot of actors," growled Uncle Luis.

Helena peered through the draped curtains from the hallway. What fun to visit Jack Swan's theater, which would be the First Theater of California! Entering the *sala*, she said, "Uncle Luis, Senor O'Brien has taught me all these songs, which I could sing in the new theater."

"Well," responded Uncle Luis, "I certainly don't want any of my daughters taking part in this kind of thing. Too much drinking at Swan's place. Helena thinks she wants to be an actress. I don't know what has got into her head. Her mother was such a peaceful person."

"There's no harm in seeing how a stage is put together. The actors are working on the platform today. They hope to construct some wings so that the performers are able to make a proper entrance," said Patrick O'Brien.

"All that minstrel stuff! That doesn't interest me a bit. Ever since the Americans have come here, we have almost forgotten our Mexican fiestas," replied Uncle Luis.

Helena went over to kiss Uncle Luis before he made for the door.

Senor O'Brien and Helena walked down Alvarado

Street past the Custom House to Mr. Jack Swan's theater. The streets were full of English-speaking strangers who had come for the Constitutional Convention.

Finally, they arrived at Mr. Swan's adobe theatre, which seemed to have two entrances. Senor O'Brien took Helena into Mr. Swan's private quarters and introduced her to him. *What a strange accent!* thought Helena; she could hardly understand what he was saying.

"Jack Swan comes from merry old Scotland," explained Senor O'Brien. "Maybe he'll teach you one of his sailor's hornpipes." He paused, then added, "But I don't think your uncle would like that."

Suddenly from another part of the house, a group of rowdy young actors dressed in old paint-streaked clothes tore into Swan's quarters. They looked at Helena and one said, "She looks like Red Riding Hood. Would make a good one."

"How about 'Goody Two Shoes'?"

"And the princess in Bluebeard's Castle?"

It was time for Senor O'Brien to speak up. "This young lady sings very well in Spanish and Russian. I am teaching her some Stephen Foster songs."

"Well, I'll be dog-blasted," said one of the actors.

"Her uncle doesn't want her to be out at night," said Senor O'Brien, "but maybe she could do a program for the children in the pueblo."

Helena was enthusiastic. "I'll get all my cousins and their friends. Maybe we could give a show on Saturday afternoon. I don't think my uncle would object to that."

The actors smiled and looked at each other. Their "Goody Two Shoes" wouldn't be able to perform at the nighttime show.

"Sing for the gentlemen," said Senor O'Brien.

Helena did. She sang her Spanish songs and then

some of Stephen Foster's American ones. When she finished, all the men had disappeared into the other part of the building. Helena guessed they didn't like her kind of singing.

"Never mind," Senor O'Brien said in a consoling voice. "We'll find some place where you can perform. Many people will like your singing and dancing . . . maybe even your Uncle Luis will some day."

"Maybe I should just forget about the stage," said Helena. "It is just too difficult."

"No," encouraged Senor O'Brien. He thought awhile. "I just remembered that Doña Josefa de Abrego has a piano, the only one in Monterey."

Helena's face brightened.

"But the trouble is, she doesn't care for strangers in her *sala*," said Senor O'Brien.

So many difficulties, thought Helena.

A Surprise

Aunt Josefa came into the kitchen, where Helena was washing the dishes. Dolores was complaining that there was grease on the platter. "The next time, Dolores, you can wash the dishes. Helena has done more than her share."

"I don't mind," said Helena. "I think about my songs or make up a story when I'm working."

Aunt Josefa took the scrub rag from Helena's hands and said, "Doña Rosalia Leese's *criada* just brought a message from her. She would like you to come right away to her house. She has a surprise for you."

"What a lovely lady!" exclaimed Helena. "She wrote all those letters for me so that I was able to come to Monterey."

Helena washed her hands and brushed her chestnut brown hair into strands, which she tied into a kind of figure eight. In several minutes she was off for the Leese *casa* on Calle Principal. When she got to the front door of a two-story frame house, she leaned down and brushed the dust from her high-button shoes.

She knocked on the door, but before anyone could open it, Helena could hear the patter of feet on the stairway inside. The patter didn't sound like a person.

The door opened . . . it couldn't be; yes, it could be! It was her old friend Pedro, and jumping up to lick her face was his wonderful sheepdog, Cano. Cano had been their special companion in Sonoma and had accompanied her to Yerba Buena, where he had been stolen.

"Oh, Cano. Oh, Pedro. I didn't think I would ever see you again!"

Pedro beamed. "But you did hear from Don Leese that

Cano found his way home to Sonoma two weeks after he was lost."

"How lucky I am!" exclaimed Helena. "To think I can see you both again!"

Cano kept jumping up on Helena and barking doglike greetings.

Senora Leese opened the door to the *sala*. "Don't knock Helena down, Cano. Be a good dog."

She turned to Helena. "I thought you would like to see your old friends and when I knew that my brother Mariano was coming from Sonoma to the Constitutional Convention, I thought he could bring Pedro with him."

"Is the great Don Vallejo staying here with you, too?" asked Helena.

"Just now he is staying with Thomas Larkin, the United States consul."

Pedro thought he had better take Cano by the collar and quiet him down. "We only got here last evening," he explained.

"This is like old times," said Helena. "You know what . . . I'm going to take you on a little trip around the town, you and Cano."

"I think that is a wonderful idea," said Senora Leese, "but do try to be here for lunch, both of you."

The fog was clearing, so there was no need of a jacket. "First, I'll take you down to the beach and then the adobe theater that I visited the other day," said Helena.

Monterey was stirring with activity. Well-dressed gentlemen, delegates to the convention, were wending their way through the dusty streets. Helena and Pedro could walk some of the time side-by-side, with Cano practically licking their heels.

"Do you suppose we'll meet Don Vallejo on his way to the convention?" asked Pedro.

"Maybe," answered Helena. "We'll go by the Thomas Larkin house and ask."

The Larkin house was larger than most, and Helena pointed out that there was a smaller house in the rear where General Sherman lived some of the time. Thomas Larkin came from New England, so he had built his house in the style of New England.

Since no one was at home, Helena escorted Pedro to the adobe theater. "I should like to be an actress and play in the theater here," said Helena.

"I don't think I would like that," said Pedro thoughtfully.

"I was hoping you would help me act out some of my songs. I want to give a program for the children of Monterey."

They stopped to look at the front of the theater but did not go inside. Helena told Pedro about Mr. Swan, the New York actors, and the fact her uncle did not want her to take part in minstrel shows.

As they walked along the beach, Helena showed Pedro the Custom House where her uncle worked as inspector. "I think we could practice down here on the beach near the wharf. You'll help me, won't you, Pedro?"

Pedro seemed a little reticent. . . . "Sure, I guess so, if Cano can be in the act. I've taught him to work on his hind legs."

"How wonderful!" exclaimed Helena. "That will make our show more attractive. Now I'm going to take you to Colton Hall, where the Constitutional Convention is taking place. Don Mariano Vallejo will be there."

Cano and the Constitutional Convention

Pedro was much impressed with Colton Hall. "The Reverend Colton built the hall with his own money," explained Helena in a proud tone of voice. "He is no longer the mayor of our pueblo. He founded the first newspaper in the state."

People were flocking together as they climbed the stairway of the large stone building.

"I guess anyone can listen to the delegates," said Helena. "Would you like to climb up there and go inside?"

"Sure," answered Pedro, trying to be polite.

"But first, I want to show you where there is going to be a school. It's down here on the lower floor. We don't have any lessons now because of the convention," said Helena.

You're lucky, thought Pedro. Out loud he said, "I asked my mother if I could come to Monterey with Don Mariano. Of course, my mother said yes."

As it was getting towards noon, there were now fewer people trying to get into Colton Hall to hear the delegates.

The children cautiously approached the open main door. Cano took the hint and walked solemnly behind them. Helena could see that the hall was very large, with a railing across the middle to divide the spectators from the members of the convention. The two friends tiptoed to one side of the room, where they could see the delegates sitting at four long tables.

At one table, Helena recognized Don Mariano Vallejo. How handsome he looked in a blue velvet jacket trimmed with gold braid! All the former Mexican delegates at his table were dressed rather elegantly. The delegates at the other three tables looked rather solemn, dressed mostly in black.

Helena and Pedro seated themselves in the back row and listened to the delegates speaking in English and Spanish. Helena explained that the interpreter was a gentlemen from Germany who spoke many languages. The man on the raised platform was the presiding officer while there were smaller tables for the secretaries and clerks.

"Can you understand what they're saying?" asked Pedro.

Since Helena now spoke both English and Spanish, she was able to tell him what was going on.

"They seem to be discussing slavery in the South of the United States," she said. "It seems that the Californians are all against it."

"How do you feel about it?" asked Pedro.

"I would be ashamed if they voted for it," said Helena.

"I, too," said Pedro.

Cano sat down on his haunches and surveyed the situation. It was all getting tiresome, from a dog's point of view.

Helena saw Cano sniff and turn his head to the open door. A large cat had found a new home here at Colton Hall. Cano growled and sniffed again. Pedro grabbed his collar, but it was too late. The cat was confused and made for the delegates' tables. Pedro lost his hold on the collar, and Cano was free to follow the enemy.

What's going to happen? thought Helena.

Cano leaped over the railing that divided the people from the delegates and started barking, as if he were one of the delegates, too. Whether he was proslavery or not was not Cano's problem. His problem was to catch the cat, at any cost!

What an uproar! The speaker of the house raised his gavel and made a thunderous bang on the table. The delegates all came to their feet.

Pedro crawled under the table where Don Mariano Vallejo had been sitting. He made a lunge at Cano, but the dog crawled farther to the other side. The dignified ex-general of the Mexican army spoke a few Spanish words as he peered under the table. "*Quedo*, Cano . . . *ven aqui*."

The familiar voice of Don Mariano quieted the dog. His attention turned to the handsome man in the blue velvet jacket, his old friend from Sonoma.

Pedro reached for Cano's collar and took a firm grip. Helena helped him drag Cano from under the table.

The presiding officer banged again on the table with his gavel. "All recess for lunch," he announced to the delegates.

Helena was happy to see the wonderful comandante again. He patted her on the head. "I am always *contento* to meet my Sonoma friends and dogs."

"*Muchas gracias*," said Helena.

The children and Cano returned to the *casa* of Doña Leese just in time for lunch, but Cano had to wait outside.

Planning the Daytime Show

"Remember what your uncle said, Helena. . . . No acting in the theater at night." Aunt Josefa was very definite in her statement.

"But you did say that Dolores and Maria and Carla could help us in the 'Camptown Races.' I've already taught them the song, singing la-la instead of the English words. They just have to pretend they are watching the races. Pedro and I are going to race each other. We're horses," said Helena.

"Helena, how can you two be horses? No one would believe you," replied Aunt Josefa.

"Senora O'Brien has some burlap and Senor O'Brien is going to make two horses' heads," Helena explained.

"Well, I never. . . . Your stories never end, Helena, and pray, where you are going to present these songs, since you will not be in the theater?" asked Aunt Josefa.

"I'm planning to do the show down on the beach," answered Helena. "We have the three songs and Cano is going to walk on his hind legs."

After finishing her afternoon chores, Helena approached her aunt. "I'm going to show Pedro the Custom House."

"Be sure not to bother your Uncle Luis today. He is very busy with two ships that have docked at the wharf. Maybe he won't even be at the Custom House."

Helena secretly hoped he wouldn't be there. He was

always so bossy and would tell her what to do and what not to do.

The streets were full of newcomers hurrying off to Colton Hall to hear the political jargon. She took her usual trek to the Leeses' house and found Pedro waiting for her. He was thrilled with the idea of seeing inside the Custom House.

"I want to stop off at the O'Brien *casa*," Helena said. "Senor O'Brien has not only promised to make two horses' heads for us, but he will make a sign announcing the show."

Senora O'Brien was at home and proudly displayed the two horses' heads and sign Senor O'Brien was working on. The sign said:

CHILDREN'S DAYTIME SHOW
ON THE BEACH
Stephen Foster Songs—a Dog with Tricks—
FREE FOR EVERYONE

"I do appreciate your husband's help," said Helena.

"How will you use the sign?" asked the senora.

"I'm planning a parade. Our company will march through the streets collecting children for an audience. We'll make a lot of noise on kettles and saws and lead everyone down to the beach where we will have our show."

"I do believe that is a good idea," said Senora O'Brien. "Please let me know if you need any more costumes. I would like to help out. I've got some old clothes I could make into skirts for the Stephen Foster songs. It's too bad you can't do your clog dance on the sand."

"I do thank you and Senor O'Brien for everything," said Helena.

"By the way, I have a whistle noisemaker you could use, and Patrick might loan you his Irish pipe," suggested Senora O'Brien.

Pedro liked the idea of a pipe. "I'd like to try to play that."

After practicing their horse movements on the beach, Helena explained to Pedro the history of the Custom House. As they strolled along, she said, "The Spanish built the Custom House before the Mexicans took over. Ships along the coast that wanted to trade unloaded their cargo there."

As they approached the building, Pedro said, "It's so big. It must hold a lot of things."

"Well, it's divided into two parts. One room is used for the guard corps and the other is for storage. This is where Commodore Sloat raised the American flag for the first time."

Pedro was interested in all the history. Cano wagged his tail as if he, too, understood the change of governments.

The white building stretched out like a sleeping tiger, the red-tiled roof like a huge mouth ready to devour children.

"The door to the guard corps section seems to be closed. We aren't really allowed inside," whispered Helena, "but I think we can go in here where the storeroom is."

The children stepped inside; it did seem rather gloomy. "My uncle is a customs officer," Helena explained. "He is down on the wharf today, but we can explore by ourselves."

Not a single person! Cano started sniffing something. "I think that's tobacco he smells," said Pedro. They followed the dog, and, sure enough, as the odor got more pungent, they came upon a barrel marked TOBACCO.

47

"Cano was right," said Pedro rather proudly. "He's got a good nose all right."

It was clear no one was in the dark storage room, so it was rather spooky. Huge vats, barrels, tubs, and casks were piled one on another. "Look what's written on this burlap bundle," said Helena.

Pedro squinted his eyes. "It's a lot of queer letters written all over it. Here are some more of those letters on this other bundle."

"I think it's Chinese writing," said Helena. "My uncle says the ships are bringing a lot of objects from China . . . various silks and ornaments."

It was getting darker as they progressed farther into the room. Helena wondered what had happened to Cano. They started calling and looking for him, then heard a sound of a closing door. This sent them scurrying towards the *entrada*. Pedro tried to lift the latch, but it wouldn't budge.

"Someone locked the door from the outside!" Helena cried. "Where is Cano? Oh, dear, my uncle will be angry when he finds out."

Pedro was more quiet. "There's nothing to do but wait until someone shows up. If Cano would keep on barking loud for five minutes, that might help. Where is the rascal?"

"Cano, Cano!" they both cried. "Where are you?"

No dog, no person to unlock the door. It was getting chilly, so they sat cross-armed to keep warm. Helena suggested they practice being horses, but Pedro didn't appreciate the idea. With their backs against the door, they waited. But no one came. Helena started to doze when she felt Cano's warm body snuggling up to hers. He was like a warm stove.

Two hours later they heard a key turning in the lock

and the familiar voice of Uncle Luis speaking sharply, "Come out here, Helena. What are you doing in the storeroom? We have been waiting dinner for you. It's way after time. Senora Leese stopped by, much worried, and I told her I would come down here and look for the two of you. Your aunt remembered you were going to show Pedro the Custom House."

The more he spoke, the angrier he got. Uncle Luis said he was tired from work and was looking forward to a good dinner.

"I'm truly sorry, Uncle Luis. I promise I won't ever be any trouble to you again."

"If you were mine, I'd take a switch to you. You must have too many ideas and get other people into trouble, like Pedro."

"I like getting into trouble a little, Senor. It is more interesting than just doing nothing."

Uncle Luis stormed home with Helena after they left Pedro and Cano at the Leese's *casa*.

The Rescue

The parade and performance were only five days ahead. Senora O'Brien was busy working on the costumes. The three cousins would have bright, colorful skirts and white *camisas* and they would carry parasols for the "Camptown Races" song. They would wear the same costumes while Helena sang "Swanee River." Of course she had a beautiful skirt that her mother had worn at Fort Ross. Senora O'Brien was making it over to fit her. It was a problem being both a beautiful singer and a horse.

Somehow the show needed another skit. Helena did a lot of thinking and presented her story to Pedro.

"I'm lost in the desert and trying to make my way through the hot sands with the broiling sun on my head. I'm looking for water everywhere, but there is none to be found. . . . I get weaker and weaker . . . my legs won't hold me up and gradually I sink down onto the sands."

"Are you dead?" asked Pedro.

"Well, almost . . . but I have a dream. . . . This is where you come in. You are wearing a black cape and are supposed to be Death. You approach me gradually, step by step and waving your arms about. But in the other direction are three travelers with parasols making their way across the sands. They see the poor woman—that's me—and since one of them has a jug of water, you, Death, will start to retire. The three travelers close their parasols and chase after you in a threatening way. Gradually I come back to life. . . . Maybe I could make up a rescue song, which the four of us would sing."

"That's a good story," said Pedro. "I would like to be that villain."

"You'd be a good one . . . make sort of scary gestures."

Senora O'Brien said she would somehow find some black calico and make a dark cape for Pedro. It would be something like a toreador's cape when he faced a bull in the ring.

Rehearsals went on all week on the beach. The three cousins liked carrying parasols and swaying to Helena's singing "Oh, Susanna." Pedro was enthusiastic about his part and practiced toreador movements with his new black cape.

"Did you invite Don Mariano Vallejo?" asked Helena of Pedro.

"Yes, I did. He thanks us very much and will come to our performance next year."

"I do know he is a busy man." Helena was disappointed.

Now they had to practice a new play. The whole cast enjoyed acting the story of the rescue.

"We'll just make up the words," advised Helena.

This they did. When the parade started, Helena and Pedro were wearing their horses' heads. With plenty of noise and whistle blowing, they marched single-file through the crowded streets of Monterey. Down and up Calle Principal and Alvarado Street, they wound. Helena told the children to follow them to the beach and see the show. Senor O'Brien carried the sign he had built, and he persuaded the children to come. What a noise they made, Cano barking the while!

The afternoon had started with sunshine, but a gusty wind was developing from over the bay. When the audience of some twenty children was quiet, Helena presented the Stephen Foster songs. Then Cano did his act. Now it was time for the rescue story. Helena was sorry Senor O'Brien

51

had to leave for Colton Hall to say good-bye to the delegates.

The wind increased so in strength that Helena was worried their costumes might blow off and the parasols turn inside out. They started the pantomime with Helena struggling in the sand, the figure of Death approaching in his black cape. The young audience squealed with delight. Just as the three travelers closed their parasols to strike out at Death, Helena miraculously revived.

Doing so, she looked out across the waters of the bay and saw that the sky was inky black and that huge waves were creating and breaking toward the shore. Worst of all, she saw a small boat floundering in the high tide, a man hanging onto the stern.

Meanwhile, the wind was getting so strong it seemed to scatter the children in all directions. There was no time for applause. "The waves are pushing the boat over toward the wharf! " yelled Helena to Pedro. "It looks like it will be dashed to pieces . . . and the man will be killed!"

Pedro, Helena, and Cano made for the wharf. Hoping to find help, Helena raced to a fisherman's post halfway down the pier. Fortunately, two stalwart men had not gone home. When they heard of the man's plight, they jumped into action.

They lowered a rope to the drowning man. Seeing that he had just enough strength to cling to it, the fishermen pulled him out of danger. In no time the man was lying on the pier, an open wound on his head and one arm hanging limp.

After some minutes, the poor water-logged victim was breathing easily. The fishermen said they would get him to a doctor. Relieved, Helena and Pedro left the scene, knowing they had taken part in a real rescue. In the meantime, the wind had died down considerably.

Off for Grass Valley

After the Constitutional Convention ended, the children of Monterey would go back to school in Colton Hall. That meant, alas, that Pedro and Cano would return to Sonoma with Don Mariano Vallejo. Helena could not bear the thought.

Aunt Josefa noticed her niece's unhappiness, but being a good aunt, she had looked into the child's future. She really believed Helena had talent and should be helped.

To Helena's surprise, she said one day, "Helena, I have received a letter from a dear friend who lives in Grass Valley. She is a neighbor of the famous dancer Lola Montez and spoke to her about you. Lola Montez has trained a young talent by the name of Lotta Crabtree, who is dancing in the theaters all over California and Nevada. It is possible you could have that same ability. Here in Monterey there is no one to coach you in dancing," said Aunt Josefa.

Helena wrinkled how brow. "But what would I do without you and Uncle Luis? You are my only family."

"I want to read you this letter, Helena, and then you will decide what you want to do."

The letter read:

Dear Josefa,

I would be delighted to have your niece live with me. Lola Montez has promised to coach Helena every day in her home. She is a kind-hearted lady and lives much alone, though there are always dogs and cats around her yard.

Helena could go to school here in Grass Valley while she is being coached by Lola Montez. I am delighted to be of help. Let me know when she will arrive. I suppose she'll come by stagecoach from Yerba Buena, San Francisco, as it is now called.

Your old friend,
Justina

On October 15th, when the convention ended, Helena was to travel with several delegates on the stage to San Francisco. They would see that she changed to another stage going to Grass Valley.

It had been a hard decision for her to make, but Aunt Josefa and the O'Briens had encouraged her to go. Even Uncle Luis was enthusiastic. Helena put her arms around her uncle. "I know you wanted to take a switch to me that night at the Custom House, but I do love you and I really didn't mean any harm."

For the first time, Uncle Luis kissed her, and there were tears in his eyes. As for her good friend Pedro and, of course, Cano, she wouldn't be able to see them for a while anyway. But when she became a famous singer and dancer, she would see them in Sonoma and maybe Monterey.

Uncle Luis piled Helena's luggage on top of the stage. They were all there—Uncle Luis, Aunt Josefa, the three cousins and her dear friends, Senor and Senora O'Brien.

Senor Patrick came over and whispered in her ear. "Doña Josefa de Abrego, the lady who owns the only piano in Monterey, wants to have a fiesta in your honor when you come back. She will accompany you for your songs and dances. She heard about your daytime show on the beach and how much the children enjoyed it."

What lovely friends and family! Helena waved to all of them as the horses pulled the coach out of the station. She was off for another adventure in another part of California.

The Immigrant Boy of Texas: A Boy's Life before the Civil War

The Young Immigrant

A warm summer evening and the smell of freshly baked kuchen (coffee cake) wafted from the kitchen stove: In Germany his mother had baked bread and kuchen before he had come to western Texas. Here he was, Hans Bruche, without father and mother but grateful that he had been accepted into his mother's Texas family, his father's family having migrated to Wisconsin.

"Do you want a piece of kuchen?" his cousin Gerda asked. She was thirteen years old, one year older than Hans. Although lame, she always insisted on doing her share of the farmwork in the garden and in the house. Since the German school was having vacation, Hans had more time to help his Uncle Wilhelm in the fields.

Before Cousin Gerda could give Hans a piece of kuchen, Great-aunt Sophie marched into the parlor. She looked at Hans. "Reading as usual," she said. "The *Herr Professor* is quite pleased with your advancement in his school. He says you are a good student. You are learning English very fast."

Hans was glad for the kuchen and the kind words of the old lady. "Thank you," he said.

He respected this well-disciplined aunt, who had withstood all the hardships in sailing from Germany to America. Was he not lucky to be accepted by these well-meaning people? He was trying so hard to be grateful.

Hans munched on the delicious kuchen. He wished he could forget the endless nights and days on the steam vessel *Herman*, which had brought him to New York City.

It was good to breathe the fresh Texas air after the putrid smells in the steerage compartment. He remembered the cramped positions when his boy's body screamed to run and shout. What a punishment to be squeezed into a mountain of human flesh all the way from Bremen, Germany, to New York! Two long weeks and four days!

Gerda smiled at Hans. She knew she was thinking about that fearful trip. She knew he always felt better when he talked about it. Besides, the *Herr Professor* wanted him to write about his experiences.

"Try to think about the good part of being in New York," she said.

"How can I when I saw my two parents taken to the Marine Hospital on Staten Island? Of course I was not allowed to go with them since they had contracted cholera on the ship."

"But the German Society in New York was good to you," Gerda insisted.

"*Natürlich!* After I heard of the death of both my parents, the society, as you know, wrote here to Uncle Wilhelm and Aunt Lili. Later they put me in the care of Herr Knute, who let me travel with him as far as New Orleans. 'You will have to go by yourself to Indianola,' Herr Knute said. 'Your cousins will meet you there.' "

Hans got up and went to the door, which was ajar.

"I know you are waiting for your friend Clear Sky," Gerda said. "You are impatient to go to the Indian ceremony this evening."

Great-aunt Sophie was listening to the conversation. "Clear Sky is a good boy," she said. "His father, the chief of the Comanche tribes, is well liked by the people of Fredericksburg."

Leaving the young people, Great-aunt Sophie went into the kitchen.

Gerda asked Hans, "Why don't you sit down and tell me more about the hurricane that struck the Gulf of Mexico at the time my parents were expecting to meet you?"

Instead of seating himself, Hans demonstrated the storm by tossing himself from chair to chair (the very ones Uncle Wilhelm had "carpented" for Aunt Lili's parlor). "The old vessel creaked and groaned," he shouted, "but she made it to Galveston!"

"Too late for my parents to meet you in Indianola," Gerda spoke quietly, trying to calm him.

Hans sat down. "Instead, it was the German Society that put me on the mail coach to Austin and then to Fredericksburg."

"Weren't you afraid?" asked Gerda.

"*Natürlich*, especially since I spoke hardly any English," replied Hans.

A clock on the mantel above the fireplace was ticking away the time. Then came a penetrating bird call, "Wee-wee-wee-wee-wee see-see-we-et."

"There is your friend, Clear Sky," said Gerda. "He certainly can imitate a yellow warbler."

"He is really my friend," said Hans. "Never did I think in Germany that I would have an Indian friend. Of course, we mostly make signs to each other. We say a few English words. German is Chinese to him."

"Don't forget your jacket," said Gerda, "it may be cool later on." She was almost a mother to him.

"Clear Sky will not want to come into the house. He is very shy," said Hans. "He does not understand German, though he seems to like the German people here in Fredericksburg."

59

The Mescal Ceremony

In the semidarkness, Hans saw his Indian friend, Clear Sky, standing in the shadow of the great barn. Uncle Wilhelm's shepherd dog was aware of the Indian's presence and growled his displeasure. Alex, the workhorse, let out a few neighs, probably tired from hauling Uncle Wilhelm's wagon with its load of fire logs and corn.

The German shepherd barked louder as Hans approached the barn.

"*Ruhgi!*" shouted Hans. "*Morgen* I will take you on a run; tonight I am busy."

More growls.

"You know Clear Sky; he is our friend," said Hans.

Hans was proud to know a young Comanche. Many Comanche tribes lived in Texas. They were often at war with each other or the Anglos. It was the German settlers like his relatives who seemed to get along with these tribes. They honestly believed the red skins and blacks were to be respected like white people.

"Happy to see you," said Hans to Clear Sky.

Clear Sky nodded. He was wearing a buckskin jacket and breeches that were trimmed with bright-colored beads. With great pride he displayed a fan of eagle feathers, which he carried in one hand. "For mescal ceremony. Have mescal buds in pouch."

"Can I see them?" asked Hans.

"When we get tepee," was the answer.

"Why go so early to the ceremony?" asked Hans.

60

"Long way over Guadalupe River to tepee. Father-chief wait. Say, 'Come early.'"

"When does the ceremony begin?"

"Begin midnight when Indians come. We have long walk get there."

Indeed, it was a long trek through the mesquite bushes and the tumbleweed, then across the Guadalupe River to the Indian campsite. It must have been around ten o'clock when the boys reached the first tepee. Hans had been told by his uncle that a tepee was a conical tent made of buffalo hide.

The Indians were already assembling, warriors and squaws, some of the squaws with a papoose on their backs. The men were in their buffalo robes while the women wore ornamented buckskin dresses. For the children, it was a great occasion. They were all gathering together to celebrate the mescal religion.

Hans followed Clear Sky through the entrance to the rear of the tepee. Tall for a boy of twelve, he managed to see over the Comanche heads. Clear Sky motioned for him to squat on the ground.

In a crouched position, the Indian placed his fan of eagle feathers on the ground and opened his pouch. He showed Hans the "mescal buttons" or buds of the cactus plant. A bud was like a disk about an inch and a half in diameter and a quarter of an inch thick.

Clear Sky whispered, "Mescal button like sun rays. Circle in center and white spots around."

Hans saw that some of the Indians were puzzled that a white boy was celebrating with them.

"My father special person. Say it all right you come with Clear Sky."

Hans felt much honored to be accepted by the Indians,

especially Clear Sky's father, the handsome chief with the noble mien.

"See fire mound," said Clear Sky. "Father-chief take care of fire."

Hans could see a crescent of earth about six inches high, which curved around the fire itself.

"Fire go all night. In center of fire is mescal rite," explained Clear Sky.

While Clear Sky remained quiet, Hans remembered what Great-aunt Sophie had told him about the rites: "The mescal rite is not for you, Hans. Just observe the ceremony, but do not eat the mescal buttons. If you do, they will give you a strange feeling, like floating in the air."

"It would be interesting to eat the buds just once," Hans had said.

"But the pleasure turns to pain," had added Great-aunt Sophie, "and even makes some Indians sick. You will want to observe the ceremony with Clear Sky, but I say to you, 'Don't eat the cactus buttons.' "

Hans was recalling all this valuable information when Clear Sky whispered, "Hear drum . . . rattles. You like?"

A new leader kept feeding the fire. Each Indian produced from his pouch four mescal buttons and ate them, one by one. Four seemed to be the magic number.

The smoke from the fire rose in circles, which gave Hans an eerie feeling. The Indians sat with blankets half-covering their heads. Sometimes a warrior would break into song. Singing seemed to have a quieting effect on the group.

From his crouched position, Clear Sky edged up to Hans. Reaching in his leather jacket, the Indian produced four mescal buttons, which he placed on the ground. Then to Hans's surprise, he brought out four more buttons. "Try mescal," he coaxed. "Me take. You take."

Somewhat overpowered by the chanting, which was getting louder and louder, Hans accepted the buttons. With the hypnotic sound of the drums and the rattles, he ate first one button, then two, then three, and finally four.

Gradually the tepee became a river of crimson fire and purple ashes. Hans's body began swaying toward the altar. He sensed a grandiose feeling of power, then luminous energy. He seemed to be floating through endless space.

A bizarre dream! He could feel the blood rising to his temples. What a fantastic world! He was reading parchment scripts from a holy book, as angels raised him to a throne of gold.

On and on went the beat of the drums until the sounds became hymns of praise. Hans stood, but rather wobbly, on his feet. There was no tepee, no Clear Sky, only people's laughter and joyful dancing. What should he do? Jump? Laugh? Cry? Dance?

Yes, he, Hans, must leave the warmth of the fire and the mescal ceremony. He must find his way back across the river to New Braunfels and home to Fredericksburg. Clear Sky had disappeared, and now he was free to dance his way back somewhere. But where was that somewhere?

Hans left the tepee, crawled through the dry bush, and in a short distance stumbled over a log. As he tripped, he fell to the ground. Suddenly he felt sick. His stomach ached and nausea overcame him. Staggering to his feet, he started to walk toward the river or was it a river? Anxiety and guilt overcame him. Where were his good, kind cousins and Great-aunt Sophie, who had warned him not to eat the cactus buttons?

It was five o'clock in the morning when Hans reached Fredericksburg. Ashamed and guilty, he saw his cousin Gerda waiting for him at the door of the house.

"I am sick," Hans said.

Gerda took his hand. "Hurry to your bed, Hans, before the others wake up. I have been waiting for you all night." She looked at him. "Your eyes are very strange," she said.

"It's my head," groaned Hans.

Gerda took his hand and led him to his bed in an alcove in the back of the kitchen. "*Guten Abend,*" she whispered. "Your bed is waiting for you."

Hans tumbled onto the mattress, his dream of paradise now an ugly, confused nightmare.

Free at Last

Hans was worried. For two days after the Comanche ceremony, Great-aunt Sophie had not spoken to him. Neither had Uncle Wilhelm and Aunt Lili. With a bad conscience, he went to the garden each morning to gather corn, potatoes, and other vegetables for the daily meals. He chopped down a young, scraggly live oak, which was growing too large near the house. He busied himself sawing the larger limbs into small pieces for firewood. He hoped he would be strong enough to remove the stump.

In his heart he wished he had taken Great-aunt Sophie's warning.

The next morning Clear Sky stood at his usual meeting place by the barn. He held a dead rabbit in his right hand, apparently just killed, as the blood was oozing down the soft brown fur.

"For you," said Clear Sky.

"Thanks," replied Hans.

"Feel better?"

No answer.

"Like shoot squirrels?"

Hans relented. "Uncle Wilhelm has one of those fur caps. I'd sort of like to have one, too."

"How your family?" asked Clear Sky.

"Worried. They read about the young lady from Hallettsville kidnapped by the Indians."

"Not kill girl. Keep her prison," said Clear Sky.

"It's bad to do that," said Hans. He squatted on the ground near his friend. Clear Sky moved up close to Hans.

65

"Tell you something. Know where girl is."

"Where?" asked Hans eagerly.

"Camp moved. Maybe twenty miles up river," replied Clear Sky.

Hans led Clear Sky over to the cornfield where no one could see them.

"I have an idea," he said. "I am like your brother, except my skin is white. You get me war paint to make my skin dark like yours. I wear a squirrel cap, leggings, and leather breeches. I will be a member of the Comanche tribe for a short time."

"Good thought. Rescue girl and take to Anglo village. Find home."

Hans looked at Clear Sky. "Your father may not like this. Do you dare?"

"My father good man, good chief. When white man take our land, we take white woman," answered Clear Sky.

It took a week to prepare for the raid, which would be on a Sunday when Hans was not working for his uncle. If he pretended to be sick, he would not have to attend church. Clear Sky brought the acid vegetable dye and helped apply it to Hans's face, arms, and hands. The squirrel hat of Uncle Wilhelm came in handy, as well as his hunting leggings.

Finally the boys were ready to set out across the fields. Since all the Fredericksburg people were in church, they would not be seen leaving the area. Hans could hear the congregation singing a Lutheran hymn he had heard at home in Hessen, Germany.

But he was in a different world now. He was on his way to rescue a white woman who might be killed by the Comanche tribe. He had not been able to save his mother and father, but maybe he could help save a young white woman.

66

The two boys traversed a swamp as they came near the Guadalupe River. They crossed the river above the falls at New Braunfels, then changed direction toward the new campsite of the Comanche Indians. They trudged on over the fields of mesquite hay dotted with thistles and Texas bluebonnets.

"See camp in distance," said Clear Sky. "Wait till dark when Indians round fire. Woman in tepee, my father say. Hope still there."

She is probably tied to the tepee, thought Hans.

The evening chant began, gradually becoming louder. Evidently the men had returned from the warpath. Perhaps they had been fighting the Apaches or another one of their tribes or even the Anglos. Since the Germans had made a treaty with the Comanches, they felt more or less safe.

Not a twig stirred as the boys sneaked up to the nearest tepee. Clear Sky nudged Hans and motioned him to follow inside. There was only darkness. Then to an adjacent tepee. More darkness only . . . yes, Hans could hear some quiet breathing. The form of a body stretched out on the ground was the woman who had been captured. Clear Sky took his hunting knife and cut the rope that bound the captive to a stake.

Hans whispered to the woman in English, "Follow us. Do not make a sound."

Fortunately, the chanting mounted in volume. Hans took the young woman's hand as the three walked stealthily out of the tepee. No one stopped them.

A coyote's bark in the distance. Another bark!

Step by step the three worked their way from the tepee into the brush. There was hardly a sound as they proceeded, only now and then a crackle of a dry twig. When they were out of hearing distance of the camp, the young woman spoke for the first time. "I do not know where I am or who you are." Her voice was soft and pleasant.

"We will take you to Fredericksburg, and there you will be safe," Hans said.

Tottering on the dusty tracks of wagon wheels, which had gouged out the dirt, Hans tried to keep the lady from falling.

"I am very tired," she said. "And I am very thankful."

On through the prickly thistle and tumbleweed. The lady was being brave and not complaining.

"Hold on to my shoulder," said Hans. "It will steady you."

They recrossed the Guadalupe River near New Braunfels, where they had been in the early evening. As they continued on their way, the little prairie dogs disappeared into their underground homes. A rattlesnake slithered by as a mother raccoon hurried by to protect her young.

Finally the few lights of Fredericksburg. The German immigrants were cautious, as night prowlers frequently passed through town. Not a soul was on the road, as it was almost dawn.

With the lady still clinging to him, Hans made for the Lutheran *Verein Kirche*. Close to the church was the sizable frame house of Herr Professor Schmitt. He would know what to do with the poor victim.

Hans knocked on the door with his left fist, as his right arm was still supporting the lady. They waited as someone was cautious about opening the door. Clear Sky felt he had done what he could for the lady and disappeared behind a live oak tree.

Holding a candlestick on high, a portly woman was examining the picture of Hans and the distressed woman. Hans recognized the rosy-cheeked face and roundish shape of the woman in the doorway as the *Herr Professor*'s sister. "*Herein,* Hans. What has happened? *Bitte, herein.* I will call my brother."

Hans helped the lady into the house.

She said in English, "I have been a captive of the Indians. The Indians do not like to have their land taken from them. I do not know if they wished to kill me. The Indian boy and this fine young man have rescued me."

The *Herr Professor*, having heard voices in the parlor, appeared at the doorway of his study. He addressed the lady in English with his German accent, "You will stay with us until you are well and strong."

Carl Is No Friend

Great-aunt Sophie was overjoyed when she heard how Hans and Clear Sky had rescued a lady from the Indians. Uncle Wilhelm and Aunt Lili offered the hospitality of their house, but the *Herr Professor* insisted she remain in his until she was stronger.

Hans told the family the lady's name was Elizabeth Turner and that she lived in the Anglo community of Hallettsville.

"You were so brave," confided Cousin Gerda to Hans. "Now you have another story to write about. The *Herr Professor* will be pleased."

In a few days, the villagers of Fredericksburg and New Braunfels knew of the rescue. Hans became a town hero. "Do not let this go to your head," said the wise professor, a handsome man of thirty-five years. He had seen enough of life and read enough books to give him a sensible outlook on life.

"How shall we see that Fräulein Turner gets to her kin?" asked Frieda, the professor's sister and housekeeper.

"Since there is no school during the summer months," answered the professor, "I shall accompany her to her home in Hallettsville. The freight wagon passes through here next Tuesday."

When Hans heard of the plan, he asked if he could go along. "If you wish to write another story, it is a good idea," answered the professor. "We can both accompany her to her home. The freight wagon could certainly hold one extra thin young passenger."

"Does Miss Elizabeth know of your plan?" asked Hans.

"Tonight I shall tell her, just at sunset."

Was the professor attracted to the beautiful blonde Elizabeth? Hans hoped some day he would marry a lady like Elizabeth Turner. Of course Uncle Wilhelm would have to let him take a short vacation from work. In five days, the return wagon would bring them home, depending on the freight.

Besides the daytime farm work for Uncle Wilhelm, Hans labored every night by candlelight to polish his stories. He was sure to have another when he returned from Elizabeth Turner's ranch. The next day he took some time off to replenish his writing equipment. He hurried to the village *Geschäft* to fetch more paper and pencils.

"What's your hurry?" a snarly voice interrupted his thoughts as he was about to enter the store.

Hans turned to see Carl Huff, another one of the *Herr Professor*'s good students. Carl had been the best student until Hans arrived from Germany.

"I just wanted to buy some writing paper," said Hans as he stopped on the threshold. He wanted to be polite.

"I suppose you think you are a writer," was the retort.

"Well, I'm just a beginner, I know. But it's true, I would like to work on a newspaper some day," replied Hans.

"You have to know something to do that," scoffed Carl Huff.

"That's true. But I can learn."

"Some people just think too much of themselves."

Hans decided to cut the conversation short and went into the store. Carrying his paper and pencils, he made his way to the professor's house. Frieda greeted him. She had been making over one of her skirts for Miss Elizabeth.

Wearing a calico blouse and a pair of white hose, Miss Elizabeth proudly displayed her new but old garments.

"Dear Frieda has polished my shoes so that I can hardly see the scuffs," she said. "How can I thank all of you wonderful people?"

Next Tuesday two families of Fredericksburg were much excited about Miss Elizabeth's departure. Hans, accompanied by Great-aunt Sophie, Uncle Wilhelm and Aunt Lili were the first to arrive at the freight depot. The *Herr Professor* and Frieda escorted Miss Elizabeth Turner. Gerda came a bit late with a bouquet of bluebonnets and an Indian paintbrush, which she handed to Miss Elizabeth.

The freight wagon arrived in a cloud of dust. The *Herr Professor* climbed over the driver's seat, then helped Miss Elizabeth to ascend. Hans climbed to the rear of the wagon and seated himself between two mail-bags. He had his pencils and paper in hand so as he could record any special event en route. He was relieved to have left his last story at the home of the *Herr Professor*, who had promised to read it on his return to Fredericksburg.

Nothing Is Easy

A week later, when Hans returned to Fredericksburg, he recounted this new story.

"Twenty miles before our freight wagon reached Hallettsville, we suddenly heard the wild cries of Indians. The driver pulled his team of horses to a stop as the howling braves descended on our wagon. There must have been ten or twelve of them.

"They were the Comanches, all right. I recognized the handsome chief, the father of Clear Sky. Then I saw my friend on an untamed mustang. At the same moment, he recognized me. As his horse reared up, he shouted at his father. Instantly his father and the other Indians turned their horses about and dropped their rifles on the animals' withers.

"Clear Sky rode his wild mustang up to the wagon and addressed Miss Elizabeth Turner, 'Happy you safe. Not harm you.' The mustang reared up."

"Wasn't Miss Elizabeth frightened?" asked Great-aunt Sophie.

Hans went on with his tale. "The Indians did not harm anyone and galloped away. After we reached the Hallettsville freight depot, Miss Elizabeth guided the wagon to her father's ranch a short distance away. She jumped out of the wagon and ran into the house to tell her family she was safe. She even told them that Clear Sky and I had rescued her.

"We stayed at the Turner Ranch as guests of the

family. I do believe the *Herr Professor* especially likes Miss Elizabeth. He looks at her that way."

Gerda looked at Hans.

He continued. "We enjoyed a marvelous feast of game and sweet potatoes, cabbage, fresh loaves of bread, and sweet butter. Also delicious melon."

Turning to his cousin Gerda, Hans asked, "Don't you think Miss Elizabeth Turner is very pretty?"

Gerda looked down at her poor leg, all crooked.

Hans quickly added, "But you are pretty, too, Gerda."

"You are just being nice." She changed the subject. "Are you going to add this adventure to your many stories?"

"Later. I'm waiting for the *Herr Professor* to make changes in my last story. I left it at his house."

The day after the freight wagon turned to Fredericksburg, Hans thought he should go over to the *Herr Professor*'s house to see if his teacher had had time to read it.

Frieda met him at the door.

"I'm glad you are all back home again, I must say. However, I did get some work done while my brother was away."

"I would be glad to help you anytime, Fräulein Frieda."

"I know you would, Hans. My brother is so impractical. He is good at his books, but when it has to do with repairing the chicken pens or digging in the garden, he is not much help. I thought in his absence I would have some work done to surprise him when he returned. *Ach!* What a happy man he is now, so amiable. Not that he is not good-hearted, but he does not tolerate stupid questions."

Hans thought he had better sit down. "I have such

respect for the *Herr Professor*. He is kind enough to help me with my stories."

The door to *Herr Professor*'s study flew open, and he hurried into the parlor. "Where did I put that story of Hans?" he questioned. "I know I left it on my desk before we left for Hallettsville."

"I haven't seen any story in your room. I cleaned your room well during your absence. There were no papers on your desk."

"But I remember I left them there." The *Herr Professor* hesitated as he looked at Hans in a guilty way. Then he addressed his sister. "Have you had any guests while I was away?"

"No, not really. Only several of your students helped me in the garden. They came into the house for a bit of kuchen, the two brothers Lucas and Carl Huff, all reliable boys," replied Frieda.

When Hans heard the name of Carl Huff, he suspected some foul play. "Herr Professor, I just want to say, though I don't know for sure, Carl Huff does not like me. He thinks I am a no-good writer."

The professor was visibly upset. He said, "It's hard to accuse someone with no proof."

"I can write the story over again, Herr Professor. Maybe it would be better the second time," replied Hans.

"Well, I'm going to get to the bottom of this," said the professor. "I don't want any thieves in my school."

The next day the *Herr Professor* invited Carl Huff to his house. He questioned him about the story of Hans. Carl Huff hesitated, then admitted he had taken the papers when Frieda went into the kitchen.

"I'm going to ask you to work here in my garden every Saturday until school begins. There will be no time for you to get into mischief, as you will be helping your parents the other days. Never again will I accept this kind of conduct from a student."

The professor was cold and forbidding. "Now I want you to tell me where you put those papers."

Carl Huff broke down. "I'm truly sorry. I burned them."

"You were one of my best students until Hans came to Fredericksburg. Just because he is a better student, works harder at his lessons, doesn't give you the right to behave this way. I'm expecting you to apologize to him. He is going to have to write his story all over again."

Carl Huff seemed quite sincere. "I will work for you every Saturday," he said.

The professor continued, "I expect to send Hans's story to the *San Antonio Presse* for consideration. I have already sent two others."

Hans Becomes an Indian

Hans kept busy during the summer months, working for Uncle Wilhelm. He helped Aunt Lili rid the cabbage of worms, the potatoes of those miserable potato bugs. He even tried to hand-plow the soil as Alex, the workhorse, was getting too old and would have to be sold. Then there was the rail fence, which was badly in need of repair.

As he struggled with these odd jobs, he thought about the stories he had given the professor to read. The *Herr Professor* had already sent the immigration story to the *San Antonio Presse*. It was a German-language newspaper that was popular with the Texans and was considered even superior to some of the Anglo periodicals.

At night Hans read his stories to Gerda when the rest of the family had gone to bed. She was always very attentive and even made some valuable suggestions. What would happen to dear Gerda as she got older? She was almost too good. People were not like that. Although the professor was a good man, his was a different kind of goodness. Perhaps he had learned it. Gerda was always kind, never critical of people. He found he did love her very much.

His best boyfriend continued to be Clear Sky. They fished together in the Guadalupe River and often brought home several catfish, which were handsomely prepared by Aunt Lili.

"Doesn't your tribe ever eat fish?" asked Hans. "You always give your fish to me for my family."

"My people eat buffalo meat. Hard to get. Not so many buffalo now."

"Too bad," offered Hans.

"My people not so sure of Indian territory. White man take. Comanche Indians share hunting grounds with Germans."

"Clear Sky, do you know any black man?"

"No."

"There are only five slaves in our county." Hans spoke thoughtfully. "I'd like to write about slavery."

"No good," agreed Clear Sky.

The two boys walked out to the barn. "You know, Clear Sky. I've been thinking. I would like to give your tribe something," said Hans.

"Not necessary. But having trouble getting corn. No rain."

Hans did some thinking. "I would like to take a wagonload of corn to your father."

That evening Hans waited for Uncle Wilhelm in the parlor. "Uncle Wilhelm," he dared say. "I was wondering if we could give some of our corn to the Comanche tribe."

"That's quite an idea," said Uncle Wilhelm as he looked for his wife's approval.

"They're good neighbors," said Aunt Lili.

"*Gut. Sehr gut*," added Great-aunt Sophie.

Uncle Wilhelm promised Hans some of the corn out of the crib.

Before Old Alex was sold, Hans and Clear Sky drove a load of corn to the Indian campsite where Clear Sky knew they would find his father. Chief Eaglenest welcomed them with an Indian grunt, then to Hans's surprise said in broken German, "Am content Clear Sky know you. Good friends. Happy to have corn. No rain. Everything dry."

Clear Sky looked at his father. "My father," he said, "think Hans should be Indian. Why not, Father?"

Chief Eaglenest paused before he spoke. "Call him different name. . . . Maybe Sure Foot. Tribal Council like."

Hans was thrilled to be considered an extended member of an Indian tribe. He would be happy with any name they gave him.

He drove his empty wagon home that evening, the happiest boy in Gillespie County. He would be a German-American and an Indian Comanche. If only he or the *Herr Professor* would hear from the *San Antonio Presse* about his stories. It was indeed nerve-racking.

The Immigrant Story

Besides knowing he was now part of American and Indian life, Hans was glad for other good news. The *Herr Professor* had proposed to the beautiful Elizabeth Turner, and she had accepted him. The wedding would be in Hallettsville in October when the weather was cooler. It would give Elizabeth's mother time to invite all the relatives in New Orleans, in Austin, and even in California.

The *Herr Professor*'s mind was divided between his coming marriage and the lessons he had to prepare for the winter season. He had written the *San Antonio Presse*, urging the editor to respond to the immigration story of Hans. So far there had been no answer.

It was always dear Gerda who was encouraging. "You will hear, Hans. One must be patient in this life."

Little did anyone know that her life was hanging on a thread. Hans noticed that every week she seemed to grow weaker and weaker. She never complained or asked for a doctor. One morning she could not get out of bed. Aunt Lili called to her. "Gerda, Gerda! Come and get your millet porridge. You need to strengthen yourself."

There was no answer.

"Hans, please see to your cousin. Her breakfast is waiting on the stove."

There was no need to rouse her. She had slipped quietly away, too good for this earth.

Hans was desperate. His Gerda! The only human being who understood him, in whom in could confide!

It was too weeks before Hans could put his mind and body to work in any sort of order. The house was in utter silence. No one spoke. There was nothing to say. Only why, why, why?

One day, however, a message did come by post and it broke Hans out of his tragic reverie. The letter was addressed to him from the *San Antonio Presse*. To think a special wagon had brought the letter to the post and Aunt Lili had been the messenger to hand it to him!

Hans was afraid to open the envelope.

"Why don't you tear it open?" Aunt Lili asked.

"Here's a knife," offered Great-aunt Sophie. "We are all waiting to hear the contents."

"Open it!" shouted Uncle Wilhelm.

Hans did so. Wait. It was a good letter. Yes, the newspaper had accepted his immigrant story. The letter went on to say that the paper needed an apprentice as a cub reporter. The editor would train him, teach him what he wanted to know.

"I cannot believe," said Hans.

"You must believe," said Great-aunt Sophie. "You see, there will be a place for you in San Antonio. You will have the proper education. You will have something to do that really interests you. It is a great opportunity."

Hans needed to tell the *Herr Professor* the good news. But how could he leave these good people and Clear Sky? Now that he was Sure Foot, a member of a Comanche tribe, he would be able to write about many cultures. Was he not a fortunate young man?

But his apprenticeship was not to be for the present. The next day Uncle Wilhelm, in trying to break a wild mustang to take the place of Old Alex, received a permanent injury to his back. Hans, always grateful to him, knew he had to take over the responsibilities of the farm. He would have to delay his journey to San Antonio for at least two years.

Arrival in San Antonio

Mud knee-deep! Water trickling over his buckskin boots! Hans made his way through the water-soaked Plaza of San Antonio. There seemed to be no sign of the rain stopping. What a miserable trip he had had from Fredericksburg! But he had made up his mind. He was going to be a journalist if he drowned in the attempt.

In his pocket he had the address of the German *San Antonio Presse*. The publishing house couldn't be too far. It was hard to see the buildings. No women and children about, only a few water-logged, disheveled-looking men trying to find shelter. Hans shouted at one passerby.

"Can you tell me where the *San Antonio Presse* office is located?"

No verbal answer but a hand pointed back in the direction he came from. He turned about. How could he have missed that sign? There it was, THE SAN ANTONIO PRESS, in large German script.

The rain splashed over his shoulders and ran down his back as he edged over to a frame building. A door, thank heaven! But the door was locked, and banging on it did not produce a human being. Perhaps he would find shelter in some wayside lodging. Yes, over there was a two-story building. It could be a refuge for the night. His clothes, wrapped in a solid bundle, were dripping with rainwater. But no matter. Here was a half-open door.

"Full up," said a not-too-friendly man's voice. "Turrible weather we're havin'. Sorry, cain't put you up."

"Any suggestion where I could go?" asked Hans as he

stepped inside. He looked around. There was little to recommend the place, a battered desk, a counter, several chairs, and some moth-eaten drapes that covered the high windows. The owner of the house, or whoever he was, matched the furnishings. Even his voice sounded as if it were mildewed. His beard dripped tobacco juice while a fur cap covered his long grayish hair. *Not a pretty sight,* thought Hans.

"Tell ya what," said the man. He was trying to be helpful. "Ya kin probably spend the night at the freight yard. Lots of travelers sleep in the main building thar. It'll keep ya out of the rain. Sorry I cain't help ya."

The man drew a diagram that Hans could follow. The freight yard, apparently, was not too far away and Hans felt he could locate it. The man spat into a spittoon alongside his desk. It was a good aim. "I kin share some of m'supper with ya. M'wife is over at her cousin's. Can't get home on account a this blasted storm. Glad t' have ya."

Hans appreciated the invitation. Perhaps the rain would stop, but he doubted he would ever get dry.

"I'll light the stove over t' the kitchen. M' clientele eat their vittels in their rooms. Everybody's in fer the night."

Hans followed the man to the kitchen. He helped stoke the wood fire in the iron stove. Rubbing his hands, he thought how fortunate he was to have a dry place for a short time.

By the time the two had eaten some corn and beans and he had made friends with a mangy-looking cat, Hans realized the rain had let up and he could be on his way to the freight yard. "People really sleep there?" he inquired again.

"Sure do. Lots of folks who come in from the East on their way to California spend the night. San Antonio's a stagecoach stop, also a center for the freight wagons."

Hans thanked the man, took his wet bundle with the diagram, and continued on his way through the streets. Two blocks here, three blocks there. Yes, that place over there did look like a freight yard or was it a lumberyard? There were rows of sawed lumber piled six feet high in rows running parallel to a large wooden structure.

Hans started to shiver. It was a humid evening, the month of July, but somehow he felt cold. He hoped he wasn't going to be sick. He had come all this way to learn how to be a writer. All he asked for was a decent place to sleep and eat.

Looking toward the large building, his attention was drawn to a small frame shack a few feet away. Maybe this was his haven. He opened a door and peering inside, he was astonished to see a young man stretched out on an Indian blanket on the floor. He looked at Hans. "Sorry to bother you," said Hans, "but I was looking for a place to put my head for the night."

"Well, there's room here for two," the young man offered. "I usually sleep in that large building over there, but there are so many travelers on their way to California, trying to get a wink of sleep. There's no place to go in this downpour. Anyhow, I just thought I would like to be by myself."

"Well, I don't have to stay," said Hans.

"Please do. I think a little company would do me good."

Hans shook the water from his jacket.

The man said, "I'll light the wood stove. You see, I'm in charge of the workers here at the lumberyard belonging to Herr Fleischer. He's a nice fella. He lets me run things here from the guard house."

Hans was grateful for the man's cordial behavior. Finally his luck had turned for the better. This young man might be just the person he needed, someone well acquainted with the town. "Your name?" questioned Hans.

"Willie, second son of Willie Jones, whose grandfather got himself a league of Texas land (four hundred acres) in 1827."

Hans yawned.

"I see you need some sleep. Here's a blanket. There's some corn pone in that box if you're hungry. We'll talk in the morning," said Willie.

Hans dropped his water-logged clothes at the door and put on his other damp trousers and shirt. Thank goodness, his writing materials were still dry! He then wrapped himself in the blanket and lay down. He was soon fast asleep.

Hans Meets Katie

Willie insisted that Hans stay with him in the guard house until he was assured of a job. After two days, when the streets were in a passable condition, Hans set out to meet his new boss. He had been assure by Willie that the lumberyard owner, Herr Fleischer, would be happy to have him stay as long as Hans wished. It was a comfortable feeling, to be sure.

However, Herr Klauss, the elderly owner and publisher of the *San Antonio Presse*, did not welcome him with open arms. He looked over his spectacles with nearsighted eyes and said, "Ya, I did write to you two years ago that I could use you here, but we are having financial troubles and the weather is so bad. The papers were not delivered on time and some did not get on the mail coach. I can only use you as a copy boy and courier. Herr Braun, my city editor, will help you get started. Here he comes now."

Hans could see that Herr Braun was a middle-aged, pompous man with a sour expression.

"This is our new copy boy and courier," Herr Klauss announced.

"Glad to know you," said Hans. "I hope I will prove to be satisfactory."

"There is nothing satisfactory in this muddy town," growled Otto Braun.

Herr Klauss tried to brighten the conversation. "A tall, good-looking blonde *Knabe* should impress our clientele. He even has German blue eyes."

Herr Braun had nothing to add to this remark.

Herr Klauss looked at Hans and continued, "Our paper is published weekly. As a copy boy and courier, you must be sure that each member of the German colony receives our journal. Over on that long table is a stack of back numbers, which came off the press a week ago. We have not been able to deliver these papers."

"I will begin work any time you wish," said Hans, trying to be enthusiastic.

Her Klauss continued, "Each paper must reach its proper destination. I hope, Herr Hans, that you are up to the job."

Hans did not dare to show his great disappointment. To come all the way from Fredericksburg to be a delivery boy when he had visions of reporting the news or writing an interesting and informative column! Of course, he was just a greenhorn.

"How did it go?" questioned good-natured Willie that evening.

"I delivered the papers to all the German families; at least I think I did. And," Hans continued, "the prettiest girl came to one door and smiled at me. She lives in that biggest house—two stories, I believe."

"That's my boss's daughter—Herr Fleischer. She's mighty beautiful with those blue eyes and that golden hair." Willie was as enthusiastic as Hans.

"Perhaps being a copy boy for a time isn't so bad. I can always do some writing here in the evening. But the only trouble is that Herr Klauss didn't mention my pay. I can't live here with you forever, and I have to buy my meals."

"I don't think I like your Herr Klauss," said Willie.

"I like him much better than Herr Otto Braun," Hans added.

The weather continued to improve, but it was exceedingly hot, as all semitropical areas should be. To live with Willie in the guard house was like living in a shoebox. The young men shared their sausages, bread, and fruits. Willie, rounded in all directions, was always in good humor and accepted Hans as a non-paying guest.

One evening Hans returned to the guard house in an exuberant mood. "Guess what . . . I talked with her."

Willie didn't say anything.

"Did you hear me? . . . I talked to her and . . . "

"And what?" asked Willie.

"She invited me to come into the parlor. I met her mother, and I spoke German with her."

"You mean with the mother?"

"Of course. Katie was born here and only knows a little German. Her mother has her tutored at home in German and English."

"Go on," said Willie.

"Well, I am invited on Sunday afternoon to meet her father, Herr Fleischer," replied Hans.

The days passed too slowly for Hans's disposition. However, there was time for Willie's aunt to wash his two shirts and underpants. He had never paid too much attention to his clothes, since he spent so much time protecting his writing materials. But it was important to look as neat as possible at the Fleischers'. The German people were sticklers for proper dress and cleanliness.

It was all a beautiful dream . . . the elegant parlor, the coffee and cream, the delicious kuchen, and of course, Katie, the lovely daughter of the house.

The conversation was half in German and half in English.

"Where are you living?" asked Frau Fleischer.

Herr Fleischer cleared his throat. "I forgot to tell you,

Liebchen, that Hans is staying with Willie in the guard house."

"But that is *zu klein* . . . too small for two young men. We must find a place for Herr Hans. . . . Indeed, we must."

"I would be most grateful, ma'am."

Suddenly Katie broke out, "I know, Mama . . . when my tutor comes, we will ask him. . . . He said something about an extra room in his boarding house." She smiled at Hans.

"That is a good idea," said Herr Fleischer. "But I must remind you that your tutor said the other day that a certain Herr Otto Braun who works for the *San Antonio Presse* was going to rent the room."

"Oh dear," sighed Katie.

Herr Fleischer stood up, which was a signal for Hans to leave.

He said most emphatically, "I will see that Herr Otto Braun has another room. I know your publisher very well. I will also see that Herr Hans has a room in the same house as Katie's tutor."

Hans did not know whether it was good or bad that Otto Braun would not have this room. He hoped Herr Otto would not try to get even with him some way.

Katie accompanied him to the outer door. Her hand caught the brass door knob just as he turned it. His eyes met hers and now, with the confidence of a man, he stepped over the threshold of the Fleischer home and made his way down the street.

The San Antonio Presse

"Herr Klauss, would you be interested in my story on Sam Houston?"

"Sorry, Hans. We have no room in our paper for biography. You write well for a young man. The *San Antonio Presse* deals with the facts of daily living. Funerals, weddings, and church affairs, mostly."

A thin nasal voice from the corner, "We already did a story on Sam Houston."

Hans retorted, "I got some more information from Herr Fleischer. He is much interested in Texas history."

"Better get going on your route, Hans." The publisher turned to pencil some data that was to be released in the paper the following week.

Hans took a small cart, which he used for delivery, and piled the periodicals inside. He needed to tie a rope around them until the pile had diminished.

"Some people need a rope around their necks," Otto snarled in a sarcastic way.

Hans said, "You know, Otto, I am really sorry about the room at Mrs. Smith's Boarding House. I think Herr Fleischer was sorry for me, as I didn't have a place to stay."

Otto broke in, "*Ja*, but he didn't need to use his influence to give you a room and take one away from me."

"*The Presse* needs the support of Herr Fleischer," said the boss.

Hans felt there was little more to say. He hoped he could do a good turn for Herr Otto Braun some day. But he wasn't going to let this situation spoil his day.

Out on to the hot streets! Past the Military Plaza and the San Fernando Cathedral . . . Civilians on horseback raced through the streets, eager to get an area where the burning hot sun did not penetrate. A coach filled with ladies and drawn by four horses ambled along. A Mexican peasant was leading, half-pulling his ox cart filled with corn and rutabaga peppers.

"Hello there, Hans" . . . a familiar voice. It was one of the Texas Rangers that he admired so much.

The ranger tried to speak a few words in German. *"Guten Tag,"* he called in his Texas twang.

"Guten Tag, yourself," called Hans. It was very pleasant to be recognized by an authority.

"On your way to the German families, I suppose?"

"Natürlich," answered Hans.

Hans was busy thinking about what he would talk about with his pretty young friend, Katie. She always waited for him at the parlor window after she had her lesson with her tutor, Timothy Thomas. It was exciting to know someone cared enough to wait for him.

Hans delivered all the papers at the end of the street and then came back to the large and impressive home of Herr Fleischer. There she was, all smiles. Hans knocked on the door and reached his hand to the floor of the wagon to take the last paper out. To his amazement, it was glued fast to the bottom.

Katie saw that something was wrong. *"Was ist,* Hans?" she asked

Katie came out and looked at the wagon.

"Who could have spilled all that glue, Hans? . . . It will be impossible to read the paper."

"I'll get you another," said Hans, quite dismayed, "but I was hoping to have a little visit."

Katie's mother called, so Katie went back into the

house to tell Frau Fleischer the news about the sticky paper. Hans hurried back to the *San Antonio Presse* and raced to the press room. Both the publisher and Otto were not there. Hans deliberated on what to do. "It looks as if I am not wanted around her," he said to himself. There was nothing to do but wait until the next day.

"I don't know how that glue could have been spilled in the wagon," said the publisher. Herr Klauss looked at Otto Braun. "*Sehr schlecht*," said Herr Klauss.

"Very strange . . . an accident, I am sure," replied Otto.

Hans was angry. "Maybe you don't care for my stories," said Hans, "but I've got a lot of ideas and I'm still going to write. Someone will like them some day."

He stormed out of the building and hurried to his new room at the boarding house. He would talk things over with his new friend, Katie's tutor.

An hour later Hans heard Timothy Thomas's footsteps in the hallway. He rushed out to meet him. "I'm sick of being pushed around," he said. "I want to publish some of my stories somewhere." He glanced at Timothy's intelligent black eyes.

"You've got some good ones." His new friend was encouraging.

"I need some money to do what I want. I'm going to ask Herr Fleischer for a job at the lumberyard. If I can make enough money, I'm going to try to buy that old press that Herr Klauss is not using at the back of his office."

"That is a very good idea," encouraged Timothy Thomas. "If you would publish in English, I could help you."

"Thank you in all languages," said Hans.

"By the way, I want you to read these two copies of the

New York Tribune. It's nice to know there are highly educated men there who publish good newspapers."

Hans was unable to sleep that night. Thoughts were fleeting through his consciousness. He wanted to speak his mind about slavery and Indian tribes. Maybe his kind of writing would not be popular with some people, but he wanted to write stories that stirred his soul.

Trouble in the Lumberyard

At long last Hans could stretch his legs under his bedroom chair and simultaneously scribble his thoughts on paper. He was pleased Herr Klauss had promised to sell him the old press. The old man realized Hans wanted to get ahead in life and that his ambition should be encouraged.

Then, too, Herr Fleischer also believed in his ability and was willing to have him assist Willie in the guard house. So much to look forward to!

There was that story of Sam Houston that Hans wanted to finish. Everyone knew Sam had come from Tennessee, that he was wounded in the Creek Indian War, that he had been governor of both Tennessee and Texas, after it had become a state. No one wrote about his youth, how he hated to go to school but loved the classics, that he wore the most outrageous clothes as a young man—a buckskin jacket trimmed with bright-colored beads and fringe, moccasin boots, and a cap with an eagle feather, which covered some of his long hair.

Sam's connection with the Cherokee tribe had always fascinated Hans. Six feet four, he towered above other men. The Indians called him "the Raven." Hans wished he could have known this brave lawyer and politician whom the Cherokees admired.

His thoughts were somewhat disturbed when Timothy Thomas came into his room. "Getting your ideas together?" questioned his neighbor.

"Yes," said Hans. "Those New York newspapers you

94

lent me are really helpful. I should be taking lessons along with Katie."

"When would you have the time, now that you are working at the lumberyard and still delivering for the *San Antonio Presse?*" asked Timothy.

"That reminds me," said Hans. "Good old Willie wants me to spend the night with him at the guard house. He's expecting trouble from some of the workers."

"Indian trouble?" asked Timothy.

"Yes. Some of the men don't want Indians working alongside of them."

"Rotten of them. Don't you think?" asked Timothy.

"The trouble is they drink too much of this homemade whiskey. The Indians and the whites get drunk—not all of them, of course."

Willie was glad to have his former roomer as a co-partner in the defense of the guard house. He handed Hans a gun but kept the rifle for himself. "You never know," he cautioned.

At midnight, when Hans was relating the story of the Comanche mescal ceremony and how he and his Indian pal had rescued a white woman, Willie signaled him to be quiet. "Hans, I think I hear footsteps."

The crunching of dry leaves outside the guard house was enough to put them on the alert. "Quick. Point your gun towards the door," came the order from Willie. "Stand back of the table!"

Poised for action, they let the seconds go by. "Aim at their legs," Willie whispered. He knew these prowlers were the dissatisfied workers who hated him. But he did not want to kill.

They waited. The door creaked and groaned and finally burst open. In the confusion, a gun was fired at Willie. The bullet missed him and grazed Hans's hand. Willie grabbed the chair and, using it as a defensive screen, charged the intruders. Hans followed. They took turns hitting the drunken leader over the head with their guns. He collapsed on the doorstep and, falling, dropped his weapon. The other three marauders, seeing their number-one man unable to fight, fled into the darkness.

"Indians or white?" asked Hans, holding his wounded left hand.

"Half-breed," said Willie, as he turned the leader over on his back.

"I'll wash your wound with some whiskey. Your hand doesn't look bad."

"What are you going to do with this mountain of flesh by the doorstep?" asked Hans.

"Just let him wear off his drunkenness. He can lie here in the dry grass until morning. I'll report the incident to Mr. Fleischer," replied Willie.

Hand-printing the Stories

Hans and Timothy Thomas enjoyed their frequent evening discussions. Articles from the *New York Tribune* were passed on to Hans and were especially coveted. But Texas history was always challenging.

"Nobody liked Santa Ana," said Hans.

"Naturally not, when you think he was responsible for the hundreds of deaths of our good Americans, also the Mexicans."

"Those men who defended the Alamo died as heroes—Davy Crockett and Col. William Travis, and others."

Hans puckered his forehead. "Of course Santa Ana was a no-gooder but a flamboyant character. Like Sam Houston, he was a born leader. I guess Santa Ana thought he was another Napoléon. Imagine his being a dictator, a general of the Mexican army, and reinstated as president five times, I believe."

Timothy was a good listener.

Hans went on. "I suppose you know the story of Santa Ana's wooden leg. If you don't, here it is. Santa Ana was wounded at San Jacinto or one of these other battles. I forget in which one he lost his leg. It had to be amputated so he had a wooden one made. Not satisfied with just one leg, he had four more designed and constructed. The leg with the fanciest decorations was to be buried at a ceremony in Mexico City. Santa Ana was to arrive with the usual pomp and formality before the leg was to be interred in the cemetery. When the people heard about the plan, they made a terrific scene and tore the leg to pieces. They were tired of this cruel dictator."

Hans and Timothy were seated in Hans's room. Suddenly Timothy stood up.

"I forgot to tell you, Hans. Mr. Fleischer wants to see you at his house."

"Tonight?" Hans asked eagerly.

Timothy nodded in the affirmative.

"It's seven o'clock right now. I'm already on my way," said Hans.

Hans was disappointed that Katie did not open the door. Herr Fleischer admitted him into the parlor. Hans always felt at home in this room, as it made him think of his cousin's parlor in Fredericksburg. The etchings and oil paintings on the wall reminded him of the family sojourn in the Black Forest of Germany when he was a little boy.

Mr. Fleischer came to the point. "I see that your hand is almost well . . . no difficulties using it, I hope. I want to thank you for helping my good employee, Willie. He thinks a lot of you, too."

"I was glad to help Willie and your company," said Hans.

"Willie tells me you would like to buy an old press from Herr Klauss. Now, do you have sufficient money?"

Hans cleared his throat.

Herr Fleischer contiuned, "Of course you don't. But I would like to help you buy this press. I am told you write very well and a bit of encouragement wouldn't harm."

Hans was quite overcome. "Oh, thank you," he said. "I am already earning some money at your lumberyard and I make a bit from the *San Antonio Presse*."

"That would probably not be sufficient," said Herr Fleischer.

Hans was disappointed not to see his dear Katie. Herr

Fleischer helped him to the door. He put a purse in Hans's hand.

"How can I ever thank you?" Hans asked.

The door was closed. He wondered why Katie did not want to see him.

Hans was able to make a down payment on the hand press. Herr Klauss was delighted to sell it, and, to the amazement of Hans, Otto smiled and congratulated him on the purchase. His lack of sincerity bothered Hans.

Good old Willie! He allowed the press to be installed in the guard house, the next day. Of course, there was now less room for Willie's clothes, his boots, and work clothes. But he believed in Hans and wanted to cooperate.

Now it was a question of hand-printing the stories. They would be in English, of course. But who would be the readers? Hans didn't know anything about circulation, and no one knew him. How would he ever get started?

That evening he sat down and talked over the matter with Timothy.

"Wonder if Herr Fleischer would have an idea," Timothy pondered.

"He's done enough for me," said Hans. He thought for a while. "You know what? . . . Since I am not publishing for money but to get writing experience and to find out if people like my work, I could maybe do this: If Herr Klauss would allow me to include my small paper with his *San Antonio Presse*, my writing would be exposed to the public."

"There would be two papers, one in German and yours in English," added Timothy.

Hans nodded in the affirmative. "Since I deliver the German papers for Herr Klauss, it would be very easy to include mine. I hope he's willing."

"This is all very well," said Timothy, "that is, if Herr Klauss agrees. What will you do for a starter?"

"I believe I'll print my Fredericksburg Indian story. I know the Americans think the Comanche tribes very dangerous. The warriors are fierce, that is true, but Clear Sky and I did rescue a white lady. Clear Sky made me one of their tribe. There are some fine Comanche Indians."

"That's a new slant on that tribe," said Timothy rather doubtfully. "By the way, Katie wants to invite you to a party at her house Saturday a week."

Hans hesitated to speak. "She seems to avoid me lately. I wonder if she doesn't care for me anymore."

"I know she likes you, Hans, but you can't be too sure of young women these days."

The Tables Are Turned

Hans had many compliments on his Indian story. Several subscribers dropped in at the *San Antonio Presse* and said as much. Many stopped him on the street.

Now it was necessary to follow up with another story with equal interest. What about his thoughts on the Negro and slavery? He had heard about the underground movement in Oberlin, Ohio. Slaves had run away and fled to the North, where black people were welcomed. Like the Germans of the nineteenth century, the townspeople believed in equality for all. Hans decided to write his views on this subject.

The following week he again distributed the papers for the *San Antonio Presse* with the additional one in English, which he called *The Spectator*. When he knocked at the Fleischer door, it was Frau Fleischer who answered.

"Katie is busy studying her English," she said in her usual motherly way. "I do hope you will come to our party next Saturday."

"Is my friend Timothy Thomas here?" asked Hans.

"He left just an hour ago, Hans," answered Frau Fleischer.

Hans decided to return the cart immediately to the *San Antonio Presse*. No one was in the bureau—not a trace of Herr Klauss or Otto Braun. Perhaps it would be a good idea to do a little writing at the guard house.

As he approached the lumberyard, he recalled the unpleasant experience with the half-breed and his group. The men had recently kept to themselves, and the half-breed always turned his face the other way when he saw Hans.

The new young publisher took out his guard house key and tried to turn the lock. It didn't respond as usual, and it was obvious Willie was not about. By pushing and shoving and wiggling the key in the lock, he finally was able to open the door.

The place seemed to be in order. He walked over to the press and examined it. But where was all the type, the metal letters? Yes, here were a few, but some of them were missing. What a fiasco! Someone must have forced the door of the guard house. That thief had waited for Willie to leave and then had deliberately stolen those letters. Without all of the type, Hans could not write and publish his stories. His head was swimming with anger, with revenge, and bitter disappointment.

Crestfallen, Hans trudged home, hoping Timothy would be there. He could then unburden his thoughts. Who could have been the thief? The half-breed would not see the value of the type. . . . There was only one real enemy, the one who was trying to be so friendly to him.

An hour later Timothy Thomas did come home. He, too, was bitterly unhappy about the situation. "Perhaps, Hans, the life here in San Antonio is not right for you. You have been struggling with your German and English languages, which now you really know quite well. But you do not know the newspaper world, journalism as it is now called. Maybe it is good that this happened because it will force you to do something else."

Hans sat down wearily on his bed. He confided to Timothy, "I didn't think I would ever want to go New York City, but since I have been reading your copies of the *New York Tribune*, I have changed my mind."

"And?" queried Timothy

Hans continued, "I read an editorial by Horace Greeley, who is encouraging young writers to try their wings."

Timothy was enthusiastic. "Then you could learn from the best teacher. What an experience that would be!"

"But what about Katie, the Fleischers?" Hans looked at Timothy who glanced away.

"Katie especially wants you to come to her party Saturday night. There will be a surprise for everyone."

"I do love her so much," said Hans, "but somehow she doesn't want to see me. I don't know why."

Timothy spoke softly. "You see, Hans, her mother and father want to announce her engagement to me. I love Katie, too. The only difference is that she seems to love me."

Hans waited before speaking. "You're the lucky one," he said quietly.

"Not necessarily. You are talented. You have a whole future ahead of you. When you are in New York you will meet the most exciting people in your trade. They will give you the experience you need."

Hans was beginning to feel better. He decided he had the best friends in the world: Willie, Katie, Timothy, Herr and Frau Fleischer, and even Herr Klauss. He was not going to think about his only enemy. He was also grateful for his loyal family and his Indian friend, Clear Sky.

On a balmy night, with the heavens filled with bright stars, Herr Fleischer announced the engagement of his daughter, Katie, to Mr. Timothy Thomas.

"And," said the indomitable owner of the lumberyard, "I want to thank our friend Hans for his interesting stories. He tells me he is bound for New York to study journalism. New York is the city where he landed six years ago as a boy immigrant from Germany. Let us drink to his success and to the health of my daughter, Katie, and her future husband!"

It would be four years before Hans would write to his friends in San Antonio and his family in Fredericksburg. By then he was a cub reporter on the *New York Tribune* and dreaming of further advancement.

Streak of Lightning; or,
An Orphan in New Mexico

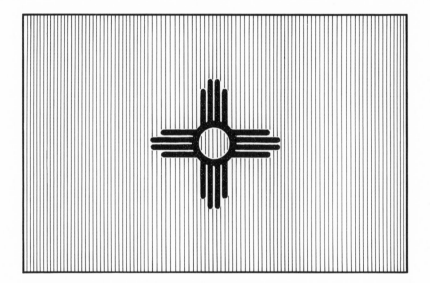

Antoinette

Nobody in Santa Fe had been quite sure what the orphan's name was until the archbishop of the diocese of New Mexico finally named her Antoinette.

"Should she have a last name to match Antoinette?" asked Mother Superior of the Sisters of Loretto.

The archbishop said, "Since she is named after my favorite cousin in Auvergne, whose birthday is in May, why not call our child Antoinette Mayo? She will be part French and part Spanish."

Mother Superior seemed quite pleased with the decision.

Antoniette Mayo's beginnings had been most unusual. Many of the people of Santa Fe knew the bizarre story of her birth. During a torrential storm, when thunder and lightning had raged through the Sangre de Cristo Mountains, a certain young woman had struggled to find shelter as she was about to give birth to a baby. After a deafening clap of thunder, so the story was told, she had been struck dead by a mighty flash of lightning.

When the storm abated, Alberto Quita, a rancher, found her body, but what was uncanny, a new-born babe lay by her side. He deftly cut the cord, took the new-born babe, whether dead or alive, to a rain barrel near his woodshed, and washed it. He then presented it to his wife.

So it was that Antoinette Mayo became another American child in the town of Santa Fe, a pueblo that had been ruled by Indians, Spanish, Mexicans, and now Anglos. The good French father, the Archbishop Lamy, had already organized a hospital, an orphanage, and even secular schools. He had been responsible for the rebuilding of the Cathedral of St. Francis and all the other churches that were in his diocese.

He was also responsible for placing Antoinette Mayo in the hands of the Sisters of Loretto. The orphanage, now a school, had been the home of the archbishop. However, he had moved to more comfortable quarters and also had a summer retreat four miles out of town in Tesuque, where he built a small chapel surrounded by many fruit trees.

It was in the patio of the orphanage where Antoinette (or Toni) liked to sit under the archbishop's wild plum tree and carve her *santos* (religious figures of wood).

The reason Toni preferred to spend her time in a quiet way was because she was lame. This imperfect baby had been born with one leg several inches shorter than the other. And so she had remained imperfect the entire ten years of her life. She could not run or chase a ball. In fact, the other girls excluded her from all their pastimes. And as she was not especially good in her studies, Antoniette felt like an outsider most of the time. She was grateful that she could spend her leisure time carving her *santos* figures.

"Why do you always carve Saint Isidore?" asked Carlotta, one of the orphans.

"Because I like him. He is good to farmers and Mexican rancheros."

Toni looked up from her work to see two of the students observing her.

"You like Saint Isidore better than Saint Joseph?" Carlotta continued to query Antoinette.

"I like Saint Isidore best of all. . . . He saved me when the lightning killed my mother," replied Toni.

"Why didn't he save your mother?" asked Carlotta.

"I guess my mother was too tired from traveling so far."

"I don't think he is a very good saint," Carlotta insisted.

"That's for sure!" Another voice from the mouth of Ana.

"I like rancheros like Alberto Quita. Maybe he doesn't pray too much, but he helps people." Toni found herself becoming quite angry with these provoking girls.

"You like Alberto!" the two girls shouted.

Getting more and more angry, Toni dropped the *santos* of Saint Isidore and raised her carving knife over her head. "I'll carve both of you to bits!" she shouted. It seemed like a streak of lightning raged through her body.

The entrance door to the patio closed with a scratchy sound. A stern voice spoke. "What is going on here in the patio, my young students?" Mother Superior was not amused.

The two girls, Carlotta and Ana, stood at attention. Toni remained defiant. She lowered her knife but remained unaffected by Mother Superior's words.

"Toni, take your *santos* and go to your room. I will see you later. As for you two girls, please begin your duties in the kitchen. Our supper will be at five o'clock, as usual."

Toni started to limp toward the door. She had her *santos* as well as the carving knife in hand. Mother Superior called after her, "Toni, you must be careful with that knife. If I see you in a temper again, I shall have to take your wood and knife from you."

One of the sisters came from the kitchen to speak to Mother Superior. "She has a bad temper, that girl," said the nun.

"It is no wonder. . . . She cannot enjoy playing games or jumping rope. Her studies do not interest her. She is a bundle of emotions that need an outlet," replied Mother Superior.

The Visitor

The following week Mother Superior had an unexpected call from Signora Trudi, a cousin of the now elderly German pianist from Wiesbaden, Germany. As usual, some of the curious students of the orphanage were on hand to welcome guests in the hall outside the formal reception room, where only adults were admitted. Toni was never among them. The young ladies curtsied and disappeared down the hall. They wondered who the smartly dressed lady could be.

"Please make yourself comfortable," Mother Superior said. She offered Signora Trudi the best chair, covered with brocade, slightly worn and of an earlier period.

"Thank you, Mother." The visitor had a strong youthful voice, with a German accent.

"I have had the privilege of meeting you at the home of your pianist cousin who has brought so much culture to our community."

"Thank you, Mother," said Signora Trudi.

"Now, what is it you wish to see me about?"

"I wanted to ask you a special favor. I am making plans for my winter kindergarten. As you may know, I have been in Santa Fe with my husband, who is occupied with our German merchandise store."

"I have heard that your new school is doing very well," Mother spoke in glowing terms.

"I want to expand my program. I feel I have much to give the children in this town, having been exposed in Germany to the best training." Signora Trudi laughed. She had that plumpness about her that sometimes makes people happy. She was the right person for small children.

Mother Superior's guest continued, "Now I shall get to the point. My husband has noticed that you have a young pupil, a lame girl by the name of Toni, who is very clever at carving *santos*. If she is capable of this kind of art work, she could probably help me with my small children—molding clay, building with wood blocks, working with different colored papers. Then, too, I would be happy to have her live in my home with my husband and myself. You see, I have no children of my own."

Mother Superior was much pleased with Trudi's plan. Here was Toni's chance to help this kind lady and to see if she had any special ability in handling young children. She thought it would be a wise step in Toni's life.

"What do you think, Toni?" Mother Superior asked the girl.

Toni was not quite sure.

Mother Superior spoke in decided tones, "We will bring your things to the signora's kindergarten school tomorrow. You will then see how you like your new home."

It was quite a long walk down Palace Street, over the river past Saint Michael's College for Boys to the two-story home of Signora Trudi. Toni had never been on the busy streets at eight o'clock in the morning. Of course, she had to walk slowly. She carried her few possessions in a kind of duffel bag.

A knock on the a solid-looking door brought Signora Trudi and a sheepdog to the door. Toni liked the dog's friendly manner.

"Don't mind Maxl," said her hostess, "he really loves everybody."

111

Maxl started to lick Toni's hand and jumped up to kiss her. *How wonderful it is to be welcomed like this!* thought Toni.

The two visitors stepped into the reception room. "Do you see one of your *santos* over the fireplace mantel?" asked Signora Trudi.

Toni was amazed. "Yes, I did carve that. . . . I gave it to one of the sisters."

"Then one of the sisters gave it to me. My husband and I prize it very highly. He would like you to carve more *santos* so that he could sell them at our merchandise store."

They were interrupted by quite a commotion, as mothers and children started to arrive for the morning session of the kindergarten. There were only eight children, around five and six years of age, mostly girls but three boys. One of the boys screamed when his mother left, but he was quieted by Signora Trudi.

I'd like to slap him, thought Toni, but she didn't say anything. She could feel her face flushed with anger.

Signora Trudi saw Mother Superior and Toni to the door.

"Toni, I have a little bed you could snuggle into," the signora said. "I would like you to live here with my husband and myself. You could help with the children in the morning, then carve your *santos* in the afternoons and evenings."

Mother Superior beamed. "This is a great opportunity for you, Toni. If it is all right with you, Signora Trudi, we will bring Toni's things here tomorrow."

Maxl raced to rub against her side. How happy Toni was to have a sheepdog for a friend!

The Miniature Clay Pueblo

Toni decided that she liked most of the children. It was fun to be in the position of authority. She found her most apt pupils were Manuel and Maria. They were able to form likenesses of Indian faces in clay. An idea came to Toni. Why not build a miniature clay pueblo? Taking courage, she spoke to Signora Trudi.

"Toni, that is a wonderful idea. All the children will contribute, and then we will invite the parents in to see their work. I am delighted with the way you handle them, especially Luis, who is such a problem." Toni remembered Luis screaming each morning when his mother left him.

Her favorite pupil was little Alberto, named after his father, Alberto Quita, who had saved her life when the lightning struck and killed her poor mother. Alberto Senior always spoke to her when he came to fetch the boy or bring a wagonload of firewood for the stoves.

The weather was getting cooler now, and Toni found herself hugging the fireplace in the evening when she was carving her *santos*. Signora Trudi's husband especially liked her Saint Isidore, the patron saint of the farmers. Most of the local artisans chose other saints to carve.

One morning rather late, when all the children had been called for, Toni realized Luis's mother had not picked him up. Signora Trudi had already left on an important errand and had told Toni to see that each child was safely in the hands of a parent.

As the front door closed on Signora Trudi, Luis ran over to Maxl and hit him. Maxl growled but did not move.

"What did you do that for?" asked Toni.

"I like to hit things," came the surly reply. Luis clenched his fist.

"If you hit me," warned Toni, "I'll hit you back." That streak of lightning was forming in her body.

"I hate you. You're ugly," yelled the youngster.

"You had better not say that again." Toni was getting more angry.

"I'll wreck your old *santos* if you touch me!"

"Just you dare!"

There was a scuffle and Luis found himself on the floor. Toni held his shoulders down and started to shake him.

An adult voice spoke. It was Luis's mother, who had slipped through the patio door. Before Toni could say a word, Luis screamed, "She hit me. She's bad!"

Luis's mother picked him up from the floor. He was not bruised in any way, but his mother kissed his imaginary hurts. "I shall certainly report this to the Signora Trudi. And, Signora Toni, don't you ever touch my child again," said Luis's mother.

Maxl came over and licked both Toni's hands. He was trying to patch up the big fight. When the door closed, leaving Toni alone with Maxl, she cried, "Oh, Maxl, I do love you. I wish the lightning would not strike me so hard."

The parents and of course the children, were much excited about the open house for the kindergarten. Even the Sisters of Loretto as well as Archbishop Lamy were invited, although the Signora Trudi didn't really expect his excellency to come to the open house.

The children had worked many mornings on the minature pueblo three stories high. Toni had carved little ladders, which she placed against the clay walls. She had

114

cut out slits in the clay for entrances and fashioned roofs of stiff paper to fit on the tops of the little apartments.

"I have invited my German pianist cousin," said Trudi to Toni, most enthusiastic. "I want you to hear her play sometime. She is an outstanding performer."

"Does she have a real piano?" asked Toni.

"Yes, she does. It came all the way from Germany. I also want to tell you a secret: I am going to have a piano here for the children so that we can sing songs from different countries. It won't be too long before the piano reaches Santa Fe."

Soon the guests started to arrive, each mother parading her own child dressed in his or her newest finery: velveteen pantaloons for the boys and bright-colored pinafores for the girls. Toni wore a new red serape that Signora Trudi had given her. She let it hang over her poor deformed foot. Even Maxl had a rose in his collar.

After the chocolate drink and the German kuchen had been served, the children sang and danced "El Lobo" and "Rosita." Toni stood at the door with Signora Trudi to say good-bye. All the parents were very proud. It was only Luis and his mother who disappeared out through the patio without a word of thanks to Signora Trudi.

"I guess your pianist cousin couldn't come," said Toni, rather sadly.

"You see, Toni, she is quite old and doesn't like crowds too much. However, I promise to take you over to her house so that she can play for you."

Confusion

The Sisters of Loretto had made several visits to see the clay pueblo. The archbishop had promised to come at his first free moment. He had been busy traveling between the many churches of his diocese. He would probably be able to see the children's accomplishment the next Tuesday.

On Monday Signora Trudi needed to see about the delivery of the piano that she could use with the children. She asked Toni to be in charge until the parents had all picked up their sons and daughters.

As soon as she had left, Luis complained, "I've got a stomach ache. Maybe I need some water."

Toni didn't believe he had a stomach ache, but she hobbled out to the cistern to get a cup full. There was Maxl chewing on her last *santo* that she had left there. She struggled to get it out of his mouth. But he decided it was a good game and chased her into the back part of the house.

After she finally retrieved it, somewhat damaged, she hurried back to the children's room. What a commotion! The clay pueblo was no more. Luis had taken the clay and was smearing it all over the faces of the little girls. He was whooping like an Indian brave, whereupon they all joined in, yelling and screaming at the top of their lungs.

In the midst of the whoopla, Signora Trudi opened the front door. She was followed by Alberto Quita, who was carrying some logs for the stoves. "What has happened, Toni?" cried Signora Trudi. "Why did you not take care of the children while I was gone? Look at this mess and the archbishop coming to see the miniature clay pueblo tomorrow. This is terrible."

Toni saw red. . . . She felt that streak of lightning going through her body. To keep from showing her intense anger, she hobbled out on the street as fast as she could manage with her twisted foot. She did not want to see those children, parents, Trudi, or anyone else.

What she did see was Alberto Quita's wagon parked in front of Trudi's kindergarten school. What a good place to hide her angry self! *I've got to get away,* thought Toni. *I cannot be here any longer.*

She managed to climb into the back end of the wagon. By edging her way to the rear of the vehicle piled high with firewood, which Alberto was delivering to the townspeople, she managed to make a kind of nest in the logs. Restacking them, she could not be seen.

Toni could hear the voices of the parents who had come to pick up their children. She heard the voice of Luis's mother, which was particularly strident. "Hurry up, Luis. Why are you so slow?"

"Bad place," said Luis. "Ugly old kindergarten!"

Then came the soft voice of Alberto Quita. "Too bad all of the children spoiled the pueblo."

"I didn't, Father," said young Alberto. "I tried to stop the children from wrecking the village."

"I hope so," said his father as he helped the boy climb into the seat beside him.

Toni didn't utter a sound, but her body was screaming defiance. She must not let Alberto Quita know of her presence. Not daring to move, for fear one of the logs might tumble, she endured her uncomfortable position. She didn't know she was in for a long ride, as Alberto was delivering a cord of wood to the Sisters of Loretto and another to Saint Michael's College for Boys. It was only during the third delivery near Alberto's ranch that he discovered the presence of Toni.

"*Hola*, what do we have here?" Then he laughed. "A girl growing out of the wood. Mama," he yelled to his wife as the mules pulled in at the ranch, "we have a young guest for the evening. It's Toni!"

Covered with sawdust, her hair all disheveled, her pinafore torn, Toni climbed down from the wagon with the help of Alberto.

"Who started the trouble at the kindergarten?" asked Alberto of his son.

"Am I supposed to tell on someone?" He waited before he spoke again. "Yes, as usual, it was Luis."

"You see," explained Toni, "he said he had a stomach ache and wanted a drink. It all happened when I was out of the room."

"And you got the blame," added Signora. "Please come right in our simple house. We are happy to have you."

Little Alberto tried to make Toni feel comfortable. "See my tiger cat-kitty. You can sleep on my bed." Toni looked at a small mattress in the corner of the kitchen.

After a simple supper of *frijoles* (beans) and *atole* (porridge), Signora Quita said, "The clouds are forming over the mountains. There will be a bad thunderstorm tonight."

Toni was happy to be safe with her good friends. Alberto Senior took her hand and led her to a wooden door facing the mountain. A gust of wind blew it open. "Out there by that large live oak tree is where I found you that stormy night," said Alberto.

Toni shivered. A crack of thunder resounded through the valley.

"Come to your mattress here by the stove," said Si-

118

gnora Quita. "This warm Indian blanket will keep you comfortable."

It was a night of confused dreams, of sudden awakenings as the thunder continued to pound the little home with threats and warnings from the heavens. A brilliant streak of lightning brought Toni to her feet. She had the sudden urge to go outside to see that big oak tree. She tiptoed over to the door and quietly lifted the latch. No one seemed to see or hear her. They were holding their hands over their ears to drown out the thunder.

As she stepped outside, the force of the wind nearly swept her off her feet. She let it blow her in the direction of the tree. Occasional streaks of lightning showed her the way, and she was grateful. She knelt down by the tree and spoke a prayer to her mother. She said from now on the streaks of lightning would not make her angry anymore. They would light her way.

In the distance she heard her name called. It was starting to rain, so she hurried back into the house as Signora Quita met her with another warm Indian blanket. "Come to sleep, Toni," said the signora. "Tomorrow will be a peaceful day, and we will see that you get back safely to the kindergarten."

The German Pianist

In order that Signora Trudi would not worry about Toni's absence, the entire Quita family accompanied her to the kindergarten the next day. The parents now understood the situation, and although disturbed by the behavior of their children, they realized Toni had tried her best. Luis was asked to leave the school, but not without a protest from his mother. She said she would bring the matter to the attention of the archbishop.

Instead of being angry, he was amused. He said Toni was forgiven, that she had behaved in a manner she thought best. He would be delighted to see her *santos*.

Of course, Signora Trudi felt guilty that she had left those children so long when she went to see about her new piano, which had been sent by ship around the cape to California and then by express wagon to Santa Fe.

When the Quita family drove up to the kindergarten, Alberto jumped out to tell Signora Trudi that they had the runaway.

It was the signora who ran out to the wagon and covered Toni with hugs and kisses. "Toni, the new piano will be here tomorrow and my cousin says she will be happy to give you lessons."

"I do not know if I would have any talent for the piano," answered Toni.

The following day, after the children had gone home, Signora Trudi told Toni to put on her special pinafore that she had worn for the open house.

Maxl barked his approval.

"Quiet, old friend," said Toni, stroking his shaggy hair. "You can bark at my piano playing when I learn to play for the children to sing and dance."

"Before we visit my cousin, Toni, my husband wants you to stop at the Merchandise Store. He said he would like to buy all the *santos* you carved," said Signora Trudi.

"I hope he will continue to like Saint Isidore, as he is my favorite saint. I think he saved my life when the lightning struck and killed my dear mother," replied Toni.

After a quick visit with Signora Trudi's husband, the signora looked at Toni's short leg and twisted foot. "Is it too far for you to walk to Canon Road?" she asked. "That is where my cousin, the fine pianist, lives."

They were ushered in by a *criada* into an elegant home, the finest in the city. The gracious hostess greeted them in German, then sat down at her square Steinway piano and, with her flexible long fingers, played magnificently several Chopin preludes.

Toni was ecstatic.

"More than anything else, I want to learn to play the piano."

And she did over a period of years. She remained a pupil of the German lady during this time and when she felt a streak of lightning was going to rage through her body, she played the "Revolutionary Etude" of Chopin. She had finally found her true self.

Louisiana Lullaby: The Legend of Annie Christmas

Annie-girl

There, waiting at the corner, was Renee's slave and friend, Annie-girl. A mountain of good cheer, Annie-girl measured five feet eleven in height. There was no telling what she measured around the middle.

"Chile," said Annie-girl, "you mama say t'wait for Annie after de pianer lesson. Had t' finish de chores in de kitchen. An you daddy, he be at de wharf waitin' for de steamship from St. Louis. Be home for sumpfin t'eat."

Renee hurried to catch up to her friend. "Here, take my music, Annie-girl. Madame Duvier asks if you could help her move her new French piano. She says it should be in the alcove of the music room."

"Sure will . . . helped her wid dat ol' American pianer. When she want Annie-girl t'move dat ting?"

Renee shrugged her shoulders, impatient to be getting along toward home. It was a pleasant afternoon. Just a week ago, the rains had flooded the streets, but today the magnolia bushes and azaleas were enjoying the wetness of the earth. To be a child of New Orleans was to experience suffocating heat and floodlike rains that made one's body perpetually sticky and uncomfortable.

Maybe that was why it was hard to play her mother's piano. Her fingers stuck to the keyboard. Why did Mama want her to take piano lessons and ballroom decorum anyway? Her brother, Pierre, had to take fencing. Renee guessed it was because Madame de St. Perier wanted her children to participate in the social life of New Orleans.

As the two friends proceeded down the road, they

walked past the stylish houses and gardens resplendent with sweet-smelling honeysuckle and dogwood. An orange-colored cat crossed their path.

"I wish Mama would let me have a cat," complained Renee.

"You brudder got dog. Dat's enuff animals," Annie-girl offered.

"Annie-girl, why do I have to do all of these things to please my mother? Play the piano for company and study French?"

"You French pretty good, chile. You mama from Paris. She want you t' talk her talk. She want you when you ol' enough t' trabel wid her and speak French wid her cousin in Paris."

At the next corner, the two friends turned toward Renee's home. The orange cat had disappeared.

The house of Renee's parents was elevated on a terraced ledge. Stretching its aristocratic pillars higher than many others in the neighborhood, the six of them stood like sentinels guarding a palace. The upper and lower galleries with eight-foot windows and ten-foot doors announced a house of great importance. This was the St. Periers' homestead.

Madame and Monsieur de St. Perier were leaders in the social life of New Orleans. At least, this is what Renee understood from her friend Annie-girl. As they were social leaders, much was expected of their children.

Sometimes Renee wished that she lived in the slave quarters. The children there had so much fun, playing with marbles and pieces of colored string. They laughed a lot and sang their Negro ditties. Why didn't her mother and father enjoy all their comforts? They spent so much time saying "do this" and "do that," or rather, "don't do that."

126

"There you mama waitin' fer de daughter on der verandah. Hope she not mad wid us."

Annie-girl was worried that she had been late collecting her charge.

"It's not your fault," said Renee as she advanced slowly towards her handsome, fashionable mother who was impatiently tapping the end of her parasol on the steps of the verandah.

"Bonjour, Mama!" shouted Renee.

"Not so loud, Renee. Try to speak like a lady."

Renee's mother opened the door to the main entrance of the house as Annie-girl scooted down a path towards the side of the house. "Come inside," said Madame de St. Perier. "I have something important to discuss with you."

The Unwanted Gift

There was no one in New Orleans who didn't agree that
Madame de St. Perier was one of the most gracious hos-
tesses in the city. She was certainly one of the best dressed,
as her well-constructed gowns were made in Paris and
especially designed for her when she made her frequent
visits there. They were fabricated by the Maison Goddard
and delivered to her in New Orleans by steamship several
weeks after her return home. "You have a perfect figure,"
said the director of the firm. "You should live in Paris,
where we could design many more garments for you."

Renee waited for her mother to speak to her.

"Please sit down here in the great hall for just a
moment. I want to to talk to you, not about your piano
lessons, but about a gift. Yes, it is a surprise, something
special I bought for you in Paris." Madame de St. Perier's
voice was soft, but also had a hard quality, like a banjo
with a broken string.

"Come follow me, *ma cherie*."

They walked past the parlor, with its rosewood furni-
ture and brocaded drapes, then up the circular staircase
to the elegant bedchamber of Madame de St. Perier. Renee
looked troubled.

"What is the matter, *ma petite*?" questioned Madame
de St. Perier. "I do not talk to you about your piano. I want
to show you something *exquise* that I bought for you in
Paris. It will become you nicely."

"But, Mama," said Renee. "It is not Christmas and I
do not have a present for you."

"It is not even your birthday present," Madame St. Perier continued. "Of course you are fourteen and getting older. Yes, *ma petite fille* is soon becoming a young lady . . . no longer a little girl with doll babies."

"What is it, Mama?" asked Renee, becoming a little impatient.

"Please come to my armoire here . . . Open the doors, see . . . What is it? Yes, it is for you . . . the most beautiful cape that I saw in Paris. I wanted it for my daughter."

Madame de St. Perier lifted a velvet cape with gold braid for Renee to see. It was lined with crimson silk to match the velvet. Almost regal was this article of clothing that Madame St. Perier had chosen for her only daughter. She waited for some kind of reaction.

Renee looked at the gift. She stroked the velvet. She looked at the garment inside and out. She picked it up and put it down. "I don't think I like it, Mama," was all she said. "It is not for me."

"It is for you, Renee. It will make you look beautiful for the summer quadrilles. You will wear it to the ball, and everyone will look at you."

Renee looked at her mother. "Do you think the young gentlemen will like me because I have a velvet cape?" she asked her mother.

Madame de St. Perier did not answer. "You will learn to like it, Renee. You must learn to be more charming. You are of French descent and you will know how to be stylish. You do not have to be beautiful, just have a special way of being different."

There was no arguing with her mother. Renee knew she would have to wear the cape at the next social evening when a famous band from St. Louis was going to play at the Cotillion Ball.

St. Joseph's Ball

The days passed slowly as Renee contemplated the awful moment when she would have to wear that fancy cape to the ball. Her brother, Pierre, and partner often led the grand march. Their mother was proud of his meticulous appearance. Being sure of himself, he managed to be accepted by the prettiest young debutantes in New Orleans. There was no mistake. He was a carbon copy of his father, who grew up on the Caribbean island of Martinique.

"Honey-chile," said Annie-girl. "You'se thinkin' about dat piece o' velvet you gotta wear on yer pretty shoulders?"

"I wish I didn't have to go to that stupid ball," cried Renee on the day before the affair. "My mother says I have to go. She thinks the young gentlemen will like to partner me. She doesn't know that at the last dance, I sat all by myself. You remember that, don't you, Annie-girl?"

"You sure likes to make yourself miserable, thinkin' all dis. You bigger girl now an purtier than you wuz. The boys is goin' t' like you, especial wid dat new cape you mama give you."

"I hate that cape!" exclaimed Renee. "I'd like to burn it up." She threw herself on her bed and gave in to her real feelings.

"Sh! . . . honey-chile . . . quiet yourself. Oncet you git to da ball, you leave dat ol' cape on de chair and make faces at da purtiest boy. You be de belle ob de ball."

There was no use talking or screaming. Renee had to admit her salmon-pink dress with the white sash was

130

especially attractive. It was just that her face was so plain and her hair so outlandishly straight.

The long-dreaded evening finally arrived. Renee's brother, Pierre, left the house early to call for his dance partner and his good friend Gustav. Madame de St. Perier was busy with her last-minute touch-ups in her attire. She wore her latest acquisition from Paris, her headdress having two feathers tucked in her hair, which gave her a distinctive and haughty appearance.

As usual her husband was late, as he was waiting for the merchant steamship from Pittsburgh to arrive. As the conscientious owner of a shipping company, he needed to check all the details. Finally at home, in his formal and proper attire, he must not forget his long dress-coat and Napoleon-like hat.

The festivities took place at the St. Louis Hotel-Chartres, which was the center of the social and economic life of New Orleans. It was there that slave auctions were held so that Annie-girl did not like to accompany her young charge to that building.

"Ah leave you to yourself," said Annie-girl as she backed away from the door of the hotel, remembering the occasions of the auctions. Annie was a free slave, so that she did not have to worry about her future life, but she cried inside for the blacks who were not so fortunate.

Renee heard the sound of many voices inside the building. She thought she recognized that of her brother, Pierre. If only . . . Annie disappeared in the shadows of the oak trees, so for a moment she felt quite alone. She gathered courage.

"I'll leave the cape here at the door," she told herself. "Even if I have on a party dress, I'm going to run down toward Papa's office on the wharf. He won't be there, but I can hide somewhere until the party is finished."

The wharf seemed farther away than she remembered. Having started in that direction, she felt she had to follow her plan. At least she would not have to wear that cape and have everybody laugh at her at not being asked to dance.

It had been dusk when Annie-girl left Renee at the entrance to the hotel. But now in the twilight, the buildings took on ghoulish shapes. Maybe she should have gone into the hotel by herself, but how could she have faced that room full of happy dancers?

Here she was on Decatur Street. She pulled her skirts up to her chin in order not to get them in the sticky mud. Maybe she should have brought that cape and dumped it there on the street.

Renee decided to be brave. She was on her way to her father's offices on the docks. How lonely it was at night! Hearing a drunken voice, she hurried along. Then, stumbling on a piece of lumber, she almost fell on her face. What difference did it make if her dress was all muddy and wrinkled? The important thing was to reach her father's office.

A slight rain impeded her progress. She kept slipping in the mud as she pursued her way in the dark. It seemed hours before she recognized the office of Monsieur de St. Perier, her father and owner of the Monongahela and Ohio Steamship Company.

Against the wall of the building were stacked some bales of cotton. Hiding behind them might prevent her from being soaked.

Crawling between the bales of cotton, Renee settled down, all squeezed in a lump. She could have used that silly old cape as an umbrella and made a little house for herself. Tired, she felt herself falling asleep and dreaming, yes, dreaming about dancing through the clouds all by herself with the cape turned into a beautiful parasol.

Renee didn't know that time was passing and that during the next two hours several rescue parties were looking for her. Fearful that she might have fallen in the river, Pierre and his friend Gustav had struck out for the docks and scoured the area. It was her brother who found her, a damp and wilted sister, overjoyed to see a familiar face.

"Renee . . . Mama is worried. She is furious. Everyone can't understand why you left the hotel and wandered off by yourself."

"I didn't want to wear that cape," Renee answered.

"Yes, I know. You left it at the door of the hotel. We thought some pirate had run off with you. You managed to spoil the evening for Papa and Mama. . . . I guess I'd better walk home with you. You'll have to get cleaned up and go to bed. Come along. Gustav will tell Mama that you are found. . . . I'll see you home."

From then on, Renee was grateful to her brother. He really seemed to care.

Up the River

Three weeks had passed since Renee's unhappy experience. Her mother, frightened that something fearful had happened to her daughter, was not as angry as might have been expected. She was tense and silent in the presence of Renee and never mentioned the cape, which Renee knew she had hidden in her armoire. Monsieur de St. Perier was too busy to dwell on the story of that evening and strangely enough, Pierre, who had never before been too friendly, was solicitous of her health.

"Gustav asked about you," he said to his sister. "He says you have the courage of a lioness."

"Really?" Renee was pleased that this good-looking older fellow would remember to ask about her.

"Gustav has heard you play the piano. He says it sounds better than his older sister."

Renee was sure she would practice the piano a little more so that she could keep on pleasing Gustav.

Pierre whispered, "Don't tell anyone, but Gustav wants to draw a picture of you at the piano. He's had some lessons from that New York artist. You would like the way he draws."

"Really?" said Renee, flattered that someone would want to make a drawing of her.

"Mama's going to Paris, you know. Gustav can come to the house every day after she goes. She might not think it ladylike to have you model for Gustav."

"I would like to model for him. Do you have to sit still for hours and hours?"

But the unexpected happened. Madame de St. Perier called Renee to her. She was writing at her desk in the library, overlooking the garden of azaleas and rhodo-dendrons.

"Renee, I want to tell you I have been making plans for you. I expect to sail on the new ocean steamship for Paris and will be gone a couple of months. I am worried that you will not be taken care of properly. Of course, Annie-girl will be here, but I think you should have one of the family see that you are having the proper disciplines."

Renee looked downcast.

"I will not be bringing you any gift from Paris this time," added Madame de St. Perier. "In a year or so, I will be able to take you up with me. But now, it is necessary for you to continue with your piano, your French, and your dancing lessons."

"I'll try to please you," said Renee. In her heart she hoped she could.

"Now, this is my plan. Cousin Gail, the American wife of Cousin Henri Bresson, is going to chaperone you while I am away. She is not coming to New Orleans, but you are going by steamboat to Natchez and live in their beautiful home on the hill."

Renee did not know whether to be sad or glad. "What happens to Pierre while you are gone?" Renee asked.

"Pierre is old enough and responsible enough to take care of himself."

"If I were responsible, couldn't I just stay here with Annie-girl?"

"I have arranged for Annie-girl to take you on the riverboat to Natchez. She will probably live at the planta-tion with Henri's slaves."

When Renee broke the news to Annie-girl, the black woman said, "You friend Annie-girl happy take you de riber. You mammy say we be off in tree days."

These were words of comfort for Renee.

Up the River to Natchez

Madame de St. Perier took the two travelers in her carriage to the docks. To be certain Renee had sufficient clothing for the visit, Madame had Annie-girl pack a huge trunk. Of course, there was other baggage, especially Annie's straw basket filled with her belongings. Papa came along in another gig and, like a French daddy, gave Renee a polite squeeze and a kiss on each cheek. Pierre and Gustav were late in arriving and promised to visit Renee in Natchez.

While the stevedores were loading the cotton bales and sugar cane on to the lower deck of the boat, Madame de St. Perier told Renee to improve her French, especially the verbs. She should practise the piano and be as polite as she could be. She said Cousin Gail was a gracious lady and that Renee should learn from her. They would see each other in New Orleans in three months.

Since Annie-girl was a free slave, she was allowed to travel in the same quarters of the ship as the white folks. The cumbersome steamboat gave a lurch and with its steam power broke away from the dock. With a piercing whistle, they were off and on their way up the river, passing flatboats, freight boats, and another steamship moored on the dock. Renee saw the white handkerchiefs being waved and heard Pierre and Gustav shouting "*Au revoir*" and "Bon voyage."

"Ah sure hope de steam boiler doan explode," said Annie-girl. Renee was deafened by the loud racket it was making. Staying close to her friend's warm body gave her a sense of security.

The captain of the steamboat came by to see that Renee was comfortable, since she was the daughter of a well-known steamship director. Leaning over the railing to wave at her family, Renee asked Annie-girl all about Natchez over the Hill and under the Hill. As the steamship let out its raucous whistle, Annie-girl explained to her about the town.

"You see, honey-chile, it's like two towns. Dey's de town by de riber where all de poor black folks is, de Indians, an some o' de white folks, like maybe de pirates an de whiskey lubbers. Dat's Natchez under de Hill. Den way up yonder, dey is Natchez on de Hill. Dat is where all de rich folks lib. Dey has piles o' de money. Deh is de richest folk in de state. Dat is what dey say."

"Do you think my cousins are very rich?" asked Renee.

"Eberybody on de Hill, dey is rich . . . not jes a little bit rich but rich like de kings and queens," explained Annie-girl.

Renee was full of questions. She wondered why Natchez had such a peculiar name.

"Ain't you gittin' a lil sleepy, chile? It's kinda warm in dis saloon. Anyhow dis is how de town got de name. Der were de Indians fore de white folks come—de Choctaw and de Chicksaw and de Natchez tribes. De story go dat de Great Sun ruled de Indians. He say dat when somebody poor, he marry de rich partner. De rich doan marry de rich, but dey marry de poor. Den pretty soon eberybody got pleny t'eat and nobody go hungry."

"That's a good idea," said Renee. "Where are the Natchez Indians today?"

"Dono, chile, dey has disappeared. . . . When dey is a good plan like dis, somehow de folks mess it up."

137

It was getting toward evening when the riverboat *Memphis* pulled into port at Natchez. Renee was tired and sleepy and was glad that Annie-girl could lead her across the gangplank onto the wharf. A gentleman, lady, and young girl about the age of Renee rushed forward to meet the new arrivals.

"We have been waiting anxiously for you for some time," said the lady. "Of course you must be Cousin Renee."

"We are content that you here," added the gentleman, who spoke English with a French accent. The third relative was Cousin Suzette, the only child of this couple. Renee was startled by her natural beauty and elegant attire.

"I don't look very presentable," explained Renee. "It was a hot day on the river."

"You look just fine to me," said Cousin Gail. She looked at Annie-girl.

"We appreciate the fact that you could accompany Renee to our home."

"Dat's right nice ob y'all. I ain't been here fer de long time. I war born in yer town under de Hill."

While the conversation was going on, Cousin Henri was leading the group over to an area where they could pick up Renee's large trunk and baggage.

"I think we could use two gigs," said Cousin Henri, noticing the size of Renee's trunk.

"You all jes let Annie-girl take care ob dat trunk," offered the black woman. With that, she lifted it with no effort and swung it over her shoulder.

"*Mon Dieu*, she is powerful!" Cousin Henri exclaimed.

"Ah was raised by my granny under de Hill. I'm t'home in dis here quarters. Ah kin stay right here when ah gits ma charge settled."

"You'll stay with us," said Cousin Gail, smiling. "You'll

stay up on the Hill. We have a room for you near the smokehouse where I think you will feel at home."

Renee noticed that Suzette didn't have much to say. She walked beside Renee before they climbed into the gig. Suzette's mother and father seated themselves and waited for the two girls to take their seats.

Cousin Henri called to Annie-girl, "Just follow us after you get that trunk and other baggage settled." To his wife he said, "*Je n'ai jamais vu . . .* never have I seen such a powerful woman."

Even though it was beginning to be dusk, Renee saw that they were passing through a district of tumbledown shanties. People everywhere, young, old, black, white, fat and thin. Then too, there was a peculiar odor from the streets. Perhaps it was because there had been a rainfall and the stench could not dry out.

Renee looked to see if the other gig was following. There was no need to worry as the horses were used to this route. Up a steep hill skidded the two gigs until they both finally reached a plateau.

What a difference, Natchez on the Hill! It was famous as the center of Southern elegance and the aristocratic life. The wealthy French and British found a good life here. The splendor of the mansions seemed to outdo the homes in New Orleans.

After climbing and crossing several streets, the first gig turned up a drive lined on each side with huge oaks covered with Spanish moss. This was the Bresson estate. With its Greek Doric columns, the huge mansion looked like an ancient temple.

This was to be Renee's new home.

"You must be tired. Tomorrow is another day," said Cousin Gail as she helped Renee down from the gig. A black servant rushed from the portico to assist them.

139

"Good evening, Rastus," said Cousin Henri. "Perhaps you can see to it that our friend in the other gig has quarters for the night. But first, there is the large trunk belonging to our young cousin from New Orleans."

Annie-girl had already lifted the trunk from the carriage and, holding it like a cradle, she was waiting to carry it to the assigned place.

"Law, dat woman as got de muscle," said Rastus.

With that the family entered the oversized doorway of the mansion, the Natchez cousin leading the way.

"We will all see you in the morning," said Cousin Gail. "I will have Rastus bring some hot supper to you, Renee, in your room. After that I will help you get settled. I'm sure Suzette will want to join us."

Suzette didn't say anything, but Renee was too tired to care. She just wanted to be by herself for a while and to get used to her new surroundings.

The Portrait Painter

The next morning Renee heard a knock on the bedroom door. She opened her eyes to see the morning sun streaming through the doors opening on to her balcony. Yards of dainty chintz curtains did not block the rays but only made the room look a bit mysterious. The four-poster mahogany bed had seemed like a sentinel of soldiers protecting her during the night. But she shouldn't daydream. She must see who was at the door.

It was her young and beautiful cousin, Suzette, attired in a riding habit.

"Do you ride?" asked Suzette.

"Not really. My brother does. I didn't seem to have any talent for it. Please come in and sit down," replied Renee.

"I just wanted to tell you that I ride in the morning. I thought that if you did, we could ride together."

Suzette seemed to be relieved that her cousin was not going to accompany her. "I won't stay, then," she said, backing away. "Mama and Papa are expecting you for breakfast. We have mostly fruit and grits. It's most boring."

As Suzette started to leave, Renee said, "This is a beautiful room. I want to look at all the pictures."

"Speaking of pictures, there is a young artist, an American portrait painter, who is doing my portrait. He comes every day and I have to sit for him," said Suzette.

"How exciting!" exclaimed Renee.

"It was exciting at first, but now I'm tired of holding

that same pose. Anyhow, I want to say that maybe you would like to watch him paint me."

"Yes, I would, indeed," said Renee. "I know a young man in New Orleans who said he wants to draw me playing the piano."

Suzette did not seem interested and said, "So you play the piano. We don't have one now. Mama ordered a spinet from Cincinnati, but I didn't like to play, so she gave it to the Catholic Sisters."

Renee didn't know if this was good or bad, but she said, "I would be glad to see you being painted."

With that Suzette made an abrupt exit.

Breakfast in the breakfast room was a sort of getting-acquainted exercise. Cousin Henri was gracious, offering Renee more pears, figs, and other fruit. Cousin Gail was busy fanning herself, as already the heat was somewhat stifling.

"I hope you will be happy here," she said. "I was eager to have you visit us, especially since we have a daughter about your age."

"She's out on her horse," said her proud father. "We never see Suzette in the morning. Do you ride?"

"Not really," answered Renee. "I've done more piano and . . . well, a little ballroom." She could not very well say that she was not popular with the young gentlemen. She continued, "Mama likes to have me take lessons. Our dancing master comes from Paris."

"So your mother will be in Paris shortly," said Cousin Gail. "She certainly manages to travel about."

"She brings me things," said Renee confidentially. "But I don't always like what she buys for me. The clothes are too fancy, and I don't feel like myself."

At eleven o'clock, Rastus showed Renee the anteroom where Mr. Adams had been working on Suzette's portrait.

The stand was pushed back in the corner with a black cloth over the picture. Renee, eager to peek under the cover to get a glimpse of it, then tiptoed over to the corner of the room.

"Well, well!" An unfamilar voice. It belonged to a young man, a rather handsome one, wearing a dark waxed moustache. Dressed in an artist's gown, he cut rather an interesting figure.

Renee was embarrassed to be caught prying into someone's unfinished portrait. "I just wanted to take a peek," she said apologetically.

"Well, who are you, my charming friend? I have not met you. Why have they kept you hidden from me?"

Just then the outer door to the lower gallery opened and in walked Suzette. She seemed annoyed that her cousin had made the acquaintance of Mr. Adams, her portrait painter.

"That is my cousin from New Orleans," said Suzette. "She just arrived last night by steamboat."

"You never told me that you had such an attractive cousin," said the artist.

Renee blushed, not quite believing him. Suzette ignored the remark. "How many more sittings will I have to have?" she asked the artist.

"I really can't say, but certainly several."

Suzette was the epitome of good health. Also, she was a kind of classic beauty, the shape of her head being not unlike that of the Venus de Milo. Her confidence gave her a kind of self-importance that appealed to men. No wonder an artist was interested in doing her portrait.

Renee spent the rest of the morning observing the artist at work. She listened to the complaints of her cousin, Suzette. "When are you going to finish this affair? . . . And this sitting is more than I can bear!"

143

Today Mr. Adams had been invited to have lunch with the two girls. He told them of his adventures traveling from New England, also about the stock material he carried with him. There were the already-painted ladies' busts, each in a different attire. Then there were the painted bonnets to match the dresses with no face under them. All he had to do when he was hired by some lady, was to add the face. It was an agreeable way of making a living.

But the portrait of Suzette had been commissioned. With her special beauty, he had painted her in her gorgeous blue-green gown as she sat on a settee covered with a golden cloth. He said she was the most beautiful model he had ever encountered.

Suzette smiled.

"And," said the artist, "I would like to paint this new cousin who has just arrived. She is so natural and has a lot of character."

Mr. Adams would start the portrait of Renee in Natchez and finish it later in New Orleans. Renee was sure she would prefer Gustav's drawing of her at the piano.

A New Acquaintance

Renee discovered that her basic likes were quite different from Suzette's. Her cousin's great love was horseback riding. Her friends were those young people interested in the equestrian arts.

Renee found herself delving into the books of the plantation library, most of which were in English, though some in French. She spent hours curled up in a comfortable chair, reading and putting together her own stories. She missed her piano music, but she would have that when she got home. That would be in a few weeks, according to the information Cousin Gail received from Madame de St. Perier in Paris.

Although Renee knew her mother and father would not approve, she spent a lot of time in the slave quarters, which on this plantation were very extensive. The dairy, office, and billiard hall were also part of the estate. Between the main house and the slave quarters, there were vegetable gardens and many plots of azalea and camellia bushes entwined with wisteria. The land was terraced in interesting designs at each level. Here the black children played, and here is where Annie-girl lived.

It was early afternoon when Renee sought the company of Annie-girl. "Sometimes I get lonely here in Natchez," Renee confided to her friend. "I guess I miss Papa and Mama and Pierre."

"Neber you know how much you miss dese folks 'til dey ain't around," said Annie-girl wisely.

Annie-girl looked at Renee. "You mama want you

home purty soon. Miss Gail say dis. Soon we gonna pack up an go up de riber. In de meantime when you is not posin fer dat fella an readin' you eyes sick, maybe you gonna vist dat por ol' lady what lives next to de plantation a mile down de road. You maybe bemember dat ol lady what waves at us when we pass in de carriage."

"Yes, I think I should like to visit her," said Renee.

"Her name Miss Lewellyn. De black folks say she got no servant."

Renee was contemplating Annie-girl's suggestion.

Annie-girl went on, "Nothin' like de present, chile. De ol' lady, she hab herself a plantation. De husband steal de money an' run off. Den a turrible thing happen. De plantation house catch on fire an' burn to de groun'. Miss Lewellyn move into de shotgun house what belong to de overseer on de place."

Annie-girl continued with her plan of action. "Ah'll walk you down t' the gate ob de ol' lady an you can make her a nice visit. She 'preciate dat."

It was not long before they were standing at the gate of the shotgun house. Renee pushed it. It resisted and made a terrible squeak when Annie-girl tried to open it.

"Do you think I should go into the yard?" asked Renee.

"Sure, chile. You go in. Knock on de front door an make de lady a call. She like it fine and mebbe she give you some sassafras tea or somfun."

Renee took courage and walked up to the unpainted front door. She knocked, one, twice, three times. Several minutes later the door was opened by the old lady. In her torn, brocaded gown, she peered out at her unexpected guests.

"We are neighbors," said Renee, indicating Annie-girl and herself.

146

"I'm happy to see you, my dears," said Miss Lewellyn. She smiled sweetly at her callers.

Renee hesitated. "I just live down the way with my cousins, Gail and Henri Bresson. Annie-girl and I thought it would be nice to get acquainted."

"Come in, my dears. I do not see many people, but I am especially delighted to have a relative of Henri Bresson call on me. I am not able to attend the various occasions of Natchez on the Hill. I used to do so, but you see, I am getting along in years and have to watch my health."

Renee nodded.

"Would you ladies like a cup of tea?"

Renee looked at Annie-girl, who smiled and nodded.

"Perhaps you would like to sit down, but unfortunately my chairs are being mended."

Renee saw a square table loaded with old books and magazines, all yellow with age.

"It takes me a long time to read all of this printed matter," said the old lady. "Sometimes I think I shall never get to the end, even before I . . . "

Renee knew what she didn't say but was thinking. It was just too difficult to say the word *die*.

"Yu'all sure looks fine," said Annie-girl in her cheerful way.

Renee moved towards the door. "We can come to see you several times before I go home to New Orleans."

"What a wonderful city!" said the hostess. "So many beautiful balls, such handsome young men, and lively Southern music."

"Yes," said Renee, doubtfully.

"And I do like the banjo," said Miss Lewellyn with a deep sigh. She tapped her right heel. "Yes, I did love to dance when I was a young lady. There is nothing here now, just a few old books."

147

With promises to return, Renee and Annie-girl closed the front gate.

The weeks passed at the Bresson plantation. With reading and visiting Miss Lewellyn, Renee felt more content. She would miss her cousins who were so good to her. Of course there was the beautiful Suzette and Mr. Adams, the portrait painter, who was always too friendly and said he was going to finish her portrait in New Orleans.

One bright morning Renee and Annie-girl were escorted by Cousin Gail, Cousin Henri, and Suzette Bresson to the docks of Natchez under the Hill. Renee was happy to be going home, but she was grateful to her three cousins.

Annie-girl waved "good-bye" to her plantation friends.

"Ah invites 'em," said Annie. "Dey doan hab de money t'trabel, but dey knows Ah be happy t' see 'em."

The Holidays in New Orleans

The winds and the rainstorms had subsided as the autumn celebrations of New Orleans ran their course. Renee was working hard at the piano. A private child, she felt solace in the beautiful compositions of the great composers. Her mother no longer had to tell her to practice or to remind her that it was her piano lesson day. She was content to make her pieces sound better. She also wanted the approval of Gustav, who had finished the drawing of her at the piano.

Gustav had even called for her at the time of Harvest Ball. It made her feel quite grown-up to accompany her brother's friend without a chaperone.

"Renee," said Gustav, as he closed the door of a gig. "There is a Mr. Adams who says he knew you in Natchez. He is trying to sell the idea of painting my sister's portrait to my parents."

"Oh dear," sighed Renee.

"He is going to be here at the Harvest Ball. Why do you frown, Renee?"

"I wish . . . " Renee could not find the words.

"This Mr. Adams says he has a portrait of you. I believe he wants to sell it to your parents," said Gustav.

Gustav had no more than spoken than Renee saw the artist waiting at the entrance of the hotel. How she wished the man with the waxed mustache was not there!

"Good evening," offered Mr. Adams with his soft-spoken voice. "How pleasant to meet you here in New Orleans."

Renee felt uncomfortable but answered, "Yes, indeed."

"Perhaps Miss Renee may have told you that when she was in Natchez with her cousins I started a portrait of her, which I have finally finished," said Mr. Adams.

Renee blushed. "I don't think my parents would care to buy it."

"I'd like to see it," said Gustav.

"Since I am traveling on by steamboat and leaving this very evening, I brought the portrait with me," Mr. Adams added.

"I've thought about the picture," said Renee, "and I know I do not want it. If I don't want it, my parents would not consider buying it."

"I'd like to see it," insisted Gustav.

The artist led the two young people to an anteroom, where his baggage and the portrait were being held by a black slave.

"The time involved and the materials cost me quite a lot of money," said Mr. Adams.

"Since Renee's parents did not commission you to do the portrait, there is no reason that they should buy it," replied Gustav.

While Gustav was talking, Mr. Adams took the portrait from a wooden box and held it in display for Renee and Gustav to see.

"It doesn't look like Renee," said Gustav. "I doubt that her parents would want to buy it."

"I could give them a special price," urged Mr. Adams.

"But I don't want it!" Renee lifted her voice. "I don't like it, and furthermore, I don't want you to show it to my parents!"

"Our little girl is becoming quite independent," retorted Mr. Adams in an ironic tone.

Gustav was getting angry. "Please don't talk like that,

sir. You are an unpleasant fellow, and I'd like to throw you out of this hotel!"

Mr. Adams looked as if the best thing to do was to disappear out of the building with the portrait before Gustav had a chance to harm him or the picture.

What a dreadful man, thought Renee as she saw the door of the hotel close. *He would do anything for a little money.*

Renee was old enough and wise enough to compare her friend Gustav with that scheming man with the black mustache. It turned out to be a beautiful evening as she glided over the dance floor with her handsome partner, Gustav.

The Christmas season was approaching, and New Orleans was making great preparations. The famous Christmas Ball would take place at the St. Louis Hotel on Chartres Street.

Renee was pleased with a simple frock that her mother had brought from Paris. This time her daughter would spend more time adjusting her bob-curls and choosing the right jewelry to match her lavender dress trimmed with lace and black velvet. Renee hoped Gustav would ask her to be his partner. How handsome and clean-cut he was compared to that slippery Mr. Adams!

It was Christmas Eve when this splendid affair was about to take place. Toward six o'clock, Renee was making the last touches to her toilet. Suddenly, unbeknownst to the St. Perier family, Annie-girl arrived at the rear of the main house and announced that the steamship *Savannah*, sailing from France, had just docked in New Orleans. On account of the storm at sea it was two days late. The sad story was that it was bringing as cargo hundreds of boxes

151

of Christmas toys for the children of New Orleans and Natchez.

Annie-girl was jubilant that the toys had arrived, but in despair as to how the toys could reach the children of Natchez by Christmas. Renee heard the great voice of her friend Annie-girl and hurried to the back of the house.

"Honey-chile," moaned Annie-girl. "You mammy and pappy gittin' ready for de party an Annie-girl afraid to talk wid 'em. Want to tell 'em, 'what is de chilluns in Natchez goin' t' do fer de Christmas?'"

"Oh, Annie," cried Renee. "We have to do something. Do you think my father would release one of the riverboats at this holiday time? It's after six o'clock!"

"Den what we do, chile?"

"First we have to take all the boxes of toys from the ocean steamboat and then stack them on the river flatboat."

"Guess yur daddy gonna get permission from de steamboat captain! You a chile ob my heart!" cried Annie-girl.

"Here, Annie. Take my party dress and let me wear your pinafore."

"Doan fit, chile. Make de wrap-aroun tree times."

"It's going to be fine, Annie-girl," said Renee.

"Am sayin' ma prayers. Dat's de bes idee."

Mama's little girl had overnight turned into a charging bison. In Annie's oversized apron-frock, Renee stumbled into her father's bedroom quarters and quickly told him the trouble. He was slow to respond, but when he did, he said, *"Ma petite*, I am going to put you in the employ of our shipping company."

So Renee, Papa, Pierre, Gustav, and, of course, Annie-girl hurried to the wharf. Here was Renee's plan: Annie-girl must first of all remove all those bales of cotton from the riverboat to make room for the boxes of toys while Renee, Pierre, and Gustav unloaded the boxes of toys from the ocean steamboat.

"Git ready t' unload soon as she throws out her gangplank!" yelled Annie-girl.

Annie-girl was at her best when she had a project. Laboriously she went to work like a stevedore. She lifted, she pushed, she hoisted, she pulled, she carried, she groaned, she swore. But she removed those bales of cotton. Now the river flatboat was clear to receive the boxes of toys from Paris.

"Who is going to run the barge up the river?" asked Renee.

"What you sayin', chile? Yer ol' friend Annie-girl goin' t'run de barge up de riber. GIVE ME THE ROPE AND CAST OFF!" she shouted. "May take all night, but de toys, dey git t'Natchez on Christmas Day."

The rope on her shoulder, Annie-girl started up the Mississippi River. Tugging and pulling, she started slowly, but gradually went faster and faster until she was almost in a run.

All night long until daylight, she pulled as the flatboat passed the houses on the river. On the dawn of Christmas Day, Annie-girl reached the docks of Natchez with the boxes of Christmas toys for the children. As the church bells rang out, the townspeople crowded down at the wharf to welcome Annie-girl.

"When I get de bref," said Annie-girl, "I tell de chilluns, dey got de bestest Christmas eber."

Renee had kept half of the boxes of toys for the children of New Orleans. They, too, were overjoyed with the special Christmas gifts from Paris, distributed by Pierre, Gustav, and, of course, Renee.

153

Joseph's Song: Czech Boys in Iowa

The Railroad Journey

The train bumped along. Jan was half asleep, his younger brother, Joseph, resting his head on Jan's lap. Another jerk as if the engine were mad at something! Then a loud whistle! Perhaps they were finally getting somewhere. Where was it they were supposed to get off? Yes, Calmar, Iowa. Jan reached into his pocket and took out a piece of butcher paper. Looking at the large letters, he reread the following information:

JAN BUSIK, AGED TEN

JOSEPH BUSIK, HIS BROTHER, AGED SEVEN

RELATIVES LIVING NEAR CALMAR AND SPILLVILLE

IN WINNECHIEK CO.

IF LOST, PLEASE NOTIFY GUSTI BUSIK IN CHICAGO, BALMORAL AV. 110

Jan had read this information one hundred times. He was afraid they would not get off at the right station. But what was the right station?

There had been so many changes since Aunt Gusti had kissed them "good-bye" at the Chicago depot. They had gotten off the train at Dubuque, but the conductor had yelled at them, "Git back on the train, young fellas. We're goin on to Macgregor, where you gotta change to the slow branch."

They climbed back in the passenger car again and found their seat. Little Joseph looked perplexed.

"What's the matter with the kid?" the conductor asked. "Seems to be not right in the head."

Jan felt hurt that someone would say things like that

about his brother. It was true, though, that Joseph was not like other children. He always took a long time to put his words together and when he did, the result was not a clear sentence. He did know a few words in Czech and a few more in English. What he said in a garbled manner was a mixture of both.

How far would it be to Macgregor, Iowa? What if the train didn't stop so that they could catch the one to Calmar?

"Quit worryin', young fella," advised the conductor. "Take a snooze and I'll holler when we git there where you change to the slow branch."

Jan trusted the conductor and was startled when he was waked out of a drowsy sleep. "Here, boy, take your gunnysack and catch that there train on the other track. I'll help yer brother off."

Jan heard the engine on the other track give a snort and a loud whistle. Another conductor holding a stepladder helped the boys climb up to the one passenger car on the slow branch.

"I'm—m—m hun—un—gry," said Joseph.

The boys settled down on the first seat that was vacant. A few tired-looking farmers and their wives stared at the children, wondering what they were doing traveling alone.

"Here, have an apple," said one housewife. "Take a pear fer the little one."

Jan thanked the woman as he took the fruit. Soon there were only two cores.

"H—h—home," said Joseph in his halting sort of speech.

"Not much longer," said Jan, hoping to make his brother feel better. "We'll be in Calmar pretty soon, where Uncle Frank is going to meet us."

Jan could see less and less as he looked out of the car window. He pressed his nose against the window by his seat. Yes, it was getting dusk and harder to see the scattered farmhouses and barns in the distance and along the tracks. Some looked mighty dirty, covered with soot from the railroad.

Finally Jan could hardly make out any objects. More train whistles and bumps . . . Perhaps they were getting to Calmar. The train was finally slowing up. Now he could see the boxcars and the flatcars along the railroad siding.

Still pressing his nose against the glass of the window, Jan noticed a man in a blue uniform. He was swinging a lantern as several buggies pulled up along the wooden platform. Yes, there were people at the station. Perhaps Uncle Frank would be there.

The conductor placed a kind of stool below the steps of the car so that the boys could descend. Jan adjusted the gunnysack over his shoulder as he took his small brother by the hand. Three steps down to the wooden platform, Jan released his hand as he turned to help little Joseph. "Don't be afraid," he said as he dropped the sack and held out his arms. "I'll catch you."

Joseph trusted his big brother. He jumped and almost knocked him into a baggage cart, which was carrying some trunks to the station.

"Lucky you got such a big brudder," said the conductor. "Take the little fella into the waiting room. Your folks ought-a be here pretty quick."

Jan wished the folks would be here now. It was really dark now, and none of the faces of the travelers looked very friendly.

"The waiting room's over there," said the conductor.

Jan heard the whistle, the clang, and the snort of the big engine, which was about to depart. He braced the gunnysack on his shoulder, took Joseph's hand, and moved toward the door of the passenger waiting room. Just as he did so, a large hairy hand grabbed his left one. "Where ya goin', boy? . . . Lookin' fer work in these parts? . . . I could use a couple a young un's on my farm. Mine's a good place t'be, boy. Jes you stick t' this Johnny. He see ya both git a place t'stay."

Jan didn't know what to do. He loosened the grip of the man and pulled his little brother after him, as he hurried to the other end of the waiting room. The man followed. "You skeered o'me?" asked the dirty man. Jan could see that his beard was messed up with tobacco juice and his hands were filthy with cracked skin like a crocodile.

The man grabbed Jan around the waist, but Jan loosened the hold and moved to another location. There were no other passengers in the room. The clock on the wall said eight-thirty. It was nighttime and still no one to greet them.

"Reckon yer folks has fergit ya," teased the man. "Might as well come along on m'jig. Live only a couple a miles from this here station. Could use a couple a young hands on m'farm."

"I have to wait for my uncle," said Jan. "He's going to pick us up."

Jan could hear the train whistle and the chug of the wheels as the familiar sounds of the steam engine gathered force and disappeared in the distance.

"Maybe you be settin' here all night," said the man. "Better come along with a feller what got a place fer ya t'stay."

"Thank you," said Jan, "but I promised to wait until my uncle comes."

"Pretty scarey fer ya . . . what with that coffin they

took off the train. It's here in the baggage room. I see'd the firemen carry it in."

Jan squeezed Joseph's hand. He was thankful his little brother didn't know what was going on in the baggage room of the station.

"Where's Un—un—Unkie Frank?" queried Joseph.

"He'll be here soon," said Jan with a tremor in his voice.

The station master came into the waiting room and lowered the gas lights. "Gotta be goin'," he said to the children. "Where yer folks?" Then he looked at the burly man on the other side of the room. "Better git goin', old skeezigs," he warned. "Am right tired yer hangin' around this here station."

The grubby man slithered out of the door. "Hope yer folks will git here soon," said the station master. "Ye kin slumber on them hard benches." Out he went after the burly man.

There was nothing else to do but wait for Uncle Frank. Joseph could curl up on a bench and put his curly head on the gunnysack. They could pretend they were in Chicago with Aunt Gusti.

Although it had been a warm evening, it was now becoming chilly.

"Go—go sleep," said little Joseph.

"First we sing together," said Jan. "Maybe that old Bohemian song, Aunt Gusti's favorite."

They sang the Czech words and, when they didn't know the words, just la-la-la. Soon Joseph fell asleep as he cuddled up against Jan. It was ten o'clock, a summer night in Calmar, Iowa.

Off to the Farm

"Wake up, my two fellas from Chicago!" It was a lusty voice. "Here's yer old Uncle Frank who's come mighty late to pick ya up."

Jan rubbed his eyes. He looked down at little Joseph, who was cuddled by his side. Oh, those trusting eyes!

Why was Uncle Frank so late? Didn't he know what time the train came in?

"Apolagize, m' boys," said Uncle Frank. "Glad t' see ya come to visit us. Berti, she all thrilled. . . . Sit up, fellas, and look at yer old Uncle Frank, who let ya stay here fer two hours all by yerselves."

"We kinda hoped you'd get here sooner," said Jan, "but we're sure glad t'see ya now, aren't we, Joseph?"

Joseph held on to Jan's hand and didn't answer.

"He has trouble talking," explained Jan. "Words isn't easy fer him."

"Never mind," said Uncle Frank. "Let me have yer gunnysack, and we'll climb in the old buggy t' git ya home for somethin t'eat."

"M—m—hun—gry," said little Joseph.

Uncle Frank led the two boys outside to the area where he had tied his mare to a hitching post. After throwing the bag into the buggy, Uncle Frank helped little Joseph up one step and into the buggy. Jan climbed in by himself.

"When we git goin', m'boys, I'll explain why I was so late. . . . "

"I'm glad we got off at the right station," said Jan very proudly.

"Gid-app, old girl," yelled Uncle Frank to the mare as he settled back next to Jan and little Joseph.

"Sure is fun ridin' behind a horse," said Jan.

"As I was a-sayin', m'boys, since I owe you an explanation, my bein' so late."

"That's all right," interrupted Jan. "We know you'd come sometime."

Uncle Frank repeated his words. "As I was a-sayin', Berti and me got mixed up on the calendar. I'd marked the train time with my red pencil, then somehow Berti, who doesn't see too well, covered it over with a dark-blue pencil. It looked then as if you folks was comin' on a Thursday instead of Wednesday."

"You sure got mixed up," said Jan.

"I found out about the mistake, but Berti, she had gone off with the buggy to Spillville where the ladies is havin' a choral rehearsal . . . music of our patriot, Antonín Dvořák. . . . Rehearsal was very important since Mr. Dvořák is leavin' perty soon t' git back t' New York . . . teachin' somewhere at some music school. I forget the name."

"I've heard of Mr. Dvořák," said Jan. "There's a choral society in Chicago where Czech people sing his songs. Aunt Gusti, she goes there every week."

"Ya see that it was important fer Aunt Berti to go to the rehearsal. It lasted extra long, so she was late gittin' back t' the farm. I found out the mistake and when I saw her comin' up the road, I run out, told her t' skidroo and jumped in the buggy, turnin' her around. Then I got the old girl-mare t' walk a fast clip. I'm sorry to make you fellas wait in the dark, but that's m' story and I did m'best."

"You sure did," said Jan.

"L—l—like horses," said little Joseph.

They rode in silence for a short time. Jan could see only the edge of the dirt road. He held on to Joseph's hand, which was soft and warm. After some minutes Uncle Frank spoke again.

"Berti will be awaitin' ya with some grub. Granny probably in bed. She ain't gittin any younger, but she sure kin bake the cornbread. Berti's a good cook, too. They'll see to it you git plenty t'eat."

Just talking about food made Jan's mouth water.

"You all right, Joseph? While we're ridin' along, maybe you could sing fer Uncle Frank."

The sounds that came out of the little mouth were so very sweet and clear. Yes, it was another old Bohemian melody. Jan joined in the chorus. The old mare began a brisk walk. She liked the music, too.

In a few minutes, Uncle Frank spoke again. "Guess we're here, fellas. There's Berti with a lantern lit fer ya. Whoa there, old girl," he called to the mare. "She knows where her place is in the barn."

"Got the boys all right?" queried a woman's voice. "Ya made pretty good time. Granny's in bed, but there's a hot stew on the stove waitin' fer ya. . . . Some corn out of the fields. Reckon that'll be enough with a tapioca puddin' for dessert."

The boys recognized a happy cheerful voice, one that reminded Jan of Aunt Gusti in Chicago. It was good to be at the farm after all these many hours of travel. A dog's bark came from the woodshed.

"That's Ricky, the sheepdog," said Uncle Frank.

"And here's Moppet, with all her kittens," said Aunt Berti.

They had entered the farmhouse through the kitchen.

164

In back of the stove in a basket was a mother tiger cat and two good-sized kittens.

"Guess you folks have a heap a animals," said Jan.

The two boys had a small room off the kitchen. It seemed cozier than the other rooms. Aunt Berti showed off her small pipe organ in the parlor, which was connected to the dining room. Two other bedrooms were down a hallway.

The boys got into bed after their late supper and fell to sleep immediately. The bed mattress was a bit hard, but they were too tired to care. Aunt Berti turned the wick down in the kerosene lamp when she saw the boys were safely in bed, tucked away under the sheets and quilt.

"Good night, little fellas," she said as she closed the door to their bedroom.

Living in the Country

In the morning Uncle Frank showed the boys how to pump water from the well. He showed them the wood house and the outhouse.

"What's that over there?" asked Jan of Aunt Berti.

"On the other side of the big red barn is the cornfield. Inside the building is where your uncle stores his farming equipment, and of course, there's the hay for the horse."

"And what's that?" asked Jan . . . "that wooden shed."

"That's the brickyard where yer Uncle Frank makes brick fer our sidewalks and driveway."

"Can I learn how to make a brick?" asked Jan.

"You sure can," answered Aunt Berti. "There's lots a chores t'do around here. We're mighty glad yer willin' t'work."

A call from the kitchen: "Who's messin' around with my cornbread?" queried a woman's voice.

Jan knew right away this was the voice of Granny, Aunt Berti's mother. She had been up gathering eggs before the boys got up.

"Come in the house and meet Granny," said Aunt Berti. "She's been waiting for you to come stay with us . . . counted the days when you would git here."

Jan liked the looks of the old lady. She had clear brown eyes, a distinguished aquiline nose, and a mischievous twinkle in her eyes. "Come kiss your granny," ordered the old lady.

Jan did. Joseph hung back a bit. "I'm not going to bite you," said Granny.

166

Joseph gave her a peck on the cheek.

"We'll be friends by the end of the summer. It's August now, going on into September when school starts. In the old country, we didn't have these long vacations. We had to learn everything in German and in Czech. The teachers were very strict."

Uncle Frank spoke to his wife. "Did ya hear that coyote last night?" he asked.

"I sure did. Gave me the heebie-jeebies."

"Lucky fer us, the chickens was all in the barn. Guess Ricky heard the critter. Scared 'em away. What with a flock of sheep, we sure need a sheepdog."

"Was it a wolf?" Jan asked.

"It's a coyote," answered Uncle Frank. "They're kind of related to wolves."

Jan was all ears. "I'd like to see a coyote," he said.

"Well, I'd like to shoot 'em all. Have killed two of our flock this year."

"If you see a coyote," warned Aunt Berti, "you'd better run fer your life."

"How can I tell the difference between a coyote and a police dog, the kind they have in the city?"

"Good question. Not much difference," said Uncle Frank. "Suspect some dogs have some coyote in 'em."

Jan and Joseph spent the day following Uncle Frank as he took care of the chores. He said the boys could gather the eggs in the morning. They could feed the six pigs, which would be slaughtered in the fall.

"They have slaughterhouses in Chicago," said Jan. "It's awful t'hear the poor pigs squeal."

With that Joseph made a sound like a pig.

"Joseph can imitate anything," explained Jan. "They say he has a good ear." Jan was proud of his brother's talent.

167

"You have to hear Joseph sing," said Jan. "He's much better than I am. Maybe he does stutter when he talks, but he sure can sing."

Several days passed as the boys explored the surrounding country. One morning after they had walked through the cornfield, they started to follow a brook that ran through the property. It was a kind of tributary to the Turkey River.

Jan hoped he would be able to catch some fish there. They sat down along the embankment of the narrow stream and started to take their shoes off. "Wonder if we could eat those berries," Jan asked himself. "Better not," he admonished Joseph. "Maybe they're poisonous."

"W—W—wwon't eat," said Joseph.

This is sure a good hideaway, thought Jan, *a hideaway from animals and people.*

"S—s—s—see blood," said Joseph.

"Yes, there's blood on the ground, at least something dark." Jan got up and looked behind one of the cottonwood shrubs. "Well, I never!" he exclaimed. "It's a baby dog, a pup—wounded. He's hurt, got a bruise on his leg."

The animal was unresponsive and looked appealingly at Jan.

"Poor little thing," said Jan sympathetically. "Doggie hiding from people."

Jan got a little closer to the animal. The little fellow started to whine.

"Leg hurt," said Jan.

"T—t—too bad," said Joseph.

"Don't touch," warned Jan. "May bite. Could be dangerous."

There was nothing to do but return to the house and report their finding to Uncle Frank. He dropped his milk pail and followed the boys to the stream.

168

"Boys," he said after he had a good look, "it's not a dog. It's a baby coyote. We haven't had enough rain, and the little fella was thirsty. Somehow he's wandered off from his mother."

"Take back t—t—t—mother," said Joseph.

"Can we have him for a pet?" asked Jan. "After we fix his leg?"

"Fraid not, boy. When he gets bigger, he'll eat up our sheep. Nothin' t' do but shoot the little fella."

"Shucks," said Jan. "He's such a cute little doggie."

The wounded animal seemed to know that he was being talked about. He just lay on the ground and waited for something to happen.

"I'll git m' shotgun," said Uncle Frank.

The boys did not want to be around when the shooting took place. They hurried back to the farmhouse and stuck pillows in their ears. But they did hear one shot.

"Frank must-a gotten him the first time," said Aunt Berti. She looked at the boys. "You have to git used t' farm life—not like Chicago. You'll git used to livin' here purty soon."

Walking to School

The country school began after Labor Day, when the children were no longer working for their parents in the fields. The schoolhouse was situated between Spillville and Calmar. It was a two-mile hike for the boys. Granny went with them the first day. She told them the teacher was expert in teaching singing, like the teachers in Czechoslovakia. The teacher rented a room in a farmhouse not far from Granny's place.

Granny and her husband had homesteaded on the Iowa land these many years. When her husband died, Granny had one daughter and son-in-law come to live on her farm. It was a good arrangement.

The first day the teacher, Miss Kullak, introduced the boys to the class. She told the students that Jan and Joseph came from the big city of Chicago. She didn't tell them that their mother had died and that their father had disappeared somewhere. She said, "I want you to know that Jan and Joseph are very fond of music. They sang in a children's chorus in the city."

The learning was hard for Joseph, as he could not answer the questions fast enough. Sometimes the children would laugh when he stuttered.

"He's got a good singing voice," said Jan to the teacher. "You should hear him."

Miss Kullak thought it a good idea for Joseph to perform. He might feel more comfortable if he could excel in something.

Joseph sang a Czech song, so very sweetly. The

children clapped their hands when he finished. Then he sang a song that made them laugh.

"Can you sing, too?" asked Miss Kullak of Jan.

"Not too well," admitted Jan. "But I can tell a Czech story about two characters called Intelligence and Luck."

When he had finished the story, Miss Kullak said, "You see, children, when you use your thinking, your intelligence"—she pointed to her head—"that is the best way of learning. If you just depend on luck, you will have a hard time getting along in life."

Jan and Joseph liked going to school, especially when it was time for the children to sing. The rafters of the old wooden building resounded with the happy voices of students. Every day when Jan and Joseph opened their tin lunch box, there was a special surprise from Granny.

"Why, what do you have written on that piece of paper in your lunch box?" asked Miss Kullak of Jan. "There seems to be a surprise between the bread and the hard-boiled eggs. It's all written in beautiful letters."

"We get a different poem from our granny each day," explained Jan. "She makes up poems about the sun, sometimes about the birds, sometimes about a river flowing into the ocean."

"What a lovely idea," said Miss Kullak. "Since most of us have families who have emigrated from Czechoslovakia, it is a nice reminder of the old country."

"I don't always understand what she says," said Jan, "but every day she writes something different."

The school bell sounded from the tower of the wooden building. It was the end of the afternoon session and time to go home. The children stood up in unison said, "Goodday, Miss Kullak."

"Good day and safe walk home," said Miss Kullak.

Jan and Joseph were getting used to farm life and

their surroundings. They liked to take different routes home. Today they chose a longer way, crossing over the property of three large farms. At the last farm, Jan saw the figure of a large farmer coming out of a broken-down shed. The man whistled at the boys, finally yelling, "Don't be skirred. Nobody goin t' bite ya."

The boys were on the man's property and perhaps he didn't want trespassers on his place. After all, Jan had seen a sign at the gate that said: BEWARE OF DOG. "We better go and see what he wants," said Jan.

The boys approached the man and, as they got closer, Jan saw that he was the same man who was at the railroad station. "Glad t' see ya agin," said the man. "I'm still a-lookin fer fellas t'help me at this here farm."

"Thank you," answered Jan, "but we are busy with school and helping Uncle Frank."

"But I'll pay ya, boy. Ya kin save yer money an go travelin' where ya want."

There was no reaction.

"Better look out fer the authorities. They'll pick ya up and take ya to one of them auctions fer kids that ain't got no mother and father. They's all orphans what ain't got no home."

"But we have a home," said Jan. As he backed away from the man, he thought to himself, *We are orphans and maybe the authorities will come and get us to work on a farm.*

Jan started to turn away with little Joseph. "Thank you, mister." He added, "I don't think we want to be auctioned off. Also, if I earn some money, what will I do with it?"

"Yer a smart kid," said the man. "Kin figur things out."

He made a lunge at the boys, but they dodged him and ran toward their farm as fast as they could go. They could hear the man laughing as he turned back toward his ramshackle house.

Jan took his little brother's hand. "We won't come this way again," he said. "We don't want to be auctioned off."

Jan told the story to Granny and Uncle Frank. They both said to beware of the ugly man and not to cross his property again.

Granny's Story

The beginning of September was a busy time. After school Jan and Joseph helped Uncle Frank load the hay from the fields onto a wagon. Jan was strong enough to lift a pitchfork, but Joseph just took an armful of hay and gave it to his brother to lift onto the wagon. After Uncle Frank was satisfied that the wagon was full to capacity, he called to the boys to get atop the loaded hay and ride to the barn. Once the hay was in the hayloft, it was much fun to jump up and down on it until it became nice and solid.

"Looks like Mother Cat had another batch of kittens in this box out here," said Jan. "Look at those poor little scrubby fellas, not exactly pretty!"

"She's lickin' em cl—l-l-lean," said Joseph He was beginning to say sentences without too much stuttering.

"Wanta help me feed the pigs?" asked Uncle Frank.

"Sure enough," answered Jan, as he and Joseph climbed down from the haymow.

They followed Uncle Frank to the hog house in back of the barn. "Them pigs'll eat anythin'," explained Uncle Frank. "They git fat on jist leavin's. Here, take this bucket a corn-cobs while I see to the sheep and the cattle."

Aunt Berti called from the kitchen, "Boys, ya want some fresh hot doughnuts? Just finished makin' a heap of 'em."

"Be right there!" yelled Jan. "After we quit feedin' the pigs!"

Jan emptied the bucket of corn-cobs, potato peelings, and pea shucks for the two fat pigs. Well-fed as they were, they still wanted to eat. Then he and Joseph ran into the house to get their doughnuts.

What a delicious odor! The hot grease in the large kitchen cooked them to a golden brown. Aunt Berti speared each doughnut with a long fork and placed them all on a large sheet of brown paper, which absorbed the grease. After waiting a few minutes, she quickly covered the doughnuts with powdered sugar. She handed each boy a fresh one. Nothing ever tasted so good!

"Looks like we're goin' to have a bad storm," said Granny to the folks in the kitchen. "Those black clouds tell me we've got a really bad one comin'. Maybe it'll strike after dinner. Usually does."

The boys had not yet experienced an Iowa cloudburst and thunderstorm. In fact, supper had already been served and eaten when Aunt Berti, listening to the first clap of thunder, said it was time to go to bed.

Ricky, the sheepdog, hurried to find a safe place under the kitchen table while Jan took another doughnut and ran over to Granny. He spoke in a loud clear voice: "Granny, you said you'd tell us some scary stories," he said, hopefully.

"That I did," said Granny. "I think it's all right t'tell 'em, Berti."

There was a flash of lightning, followed by a loud clap of thunder.

"I want you boys to go upstairs and each one bring down a feather pillow from the guest room. Holding on to the pillow will keep you from being struck by lightning. I'll be settin' here waitin' for ya."

Another streak of lightning! "Turn down the wick in the kerosene lamp there, Berti, and join us here on your rockin' chair. Frank, you're bein' busy with the animals, so you won't hear these old family tales."

Uncle Frank, who had been dozing, was now wide awake. "If you excuse me," he said, "I'm goin out t' see the horses are closed in and the other animals under cover."

"I'll run upstairs and get those feather pillows," offered Jan.

When he came back, Granny said, "Come a little closer, children, and I'll tell you what happened in Uncle Frank's farmhouse when Frank's mother was growing up."

Jan and Joseph sat cross-legged, each with a pillow on his lap.

"It seems Frank's granddad was buildin' a new farmhouse a mile down the road from here. Each family, at that time, was offered 160 acres of land if they had the intention of building a farm. Frank told me this story, so I'm goin t' pass it on t' you."

"Didn't they have to pay any money?" queried Jan.

"Not in this country. It was different from the countries in Europe."

Suddenly another flash of lightning came, followed by a clap of thunder. Joseph hugged his feather pillow and edged over close to Jan. Granny said, "Now, Frank's grandma had a heap o' kids, the last one bein a baby about a year old . . . They were all livin' in the farmhouse that was not quite complete, the upstairs room over the porch only havin' walls and no ceilin'. The walls run around and were about ten feet high."

"Uncle Frank showed me that house," said Jan.

"It was a good farmhouse all right for a settler, but Uncle Frank's grandma was a bit touched in the head from havin' so many kids. Anyhow, her husband, old Granddad, woke up one night t' find his wife wasn't a-bed. He gets himself a candle and finds his wife's not in the bedroom. In the corner where the crib was, the baby has disappeared!"

176

Joseph grabbed Jan's hand.

Granny took a deep breath and continued. "Uncle Frank's grandfather went into the hall and looked into the bedroom where the older children were sleeping. Still there was no Grandma. . . . But I didn't tell you this before. The house not being finished over the porch, there was a wall on four sides with no roof over it. It was goin' to be an extra room in case there were more children. . . . Now I'm goin' t' tell you what Frank's grandpa saw."

"Was it a ghost?" asked Jan.

"It was worse than that," said Granny. "Carrying the tiny baby in her arms was his wife. She was walkin' around the top of the walls in the dark!"

"Why did she do that?" asked Jan.

"Well, she was sleepwalking, didn't know what she was doin'. Frank's grandfather didn't dare say a word for fear the lady would wake up and realize what she was doin'."

"It's just somebody havin a bad dream and the dream is so strong and real that it makes the dreamer do things they don't know they're doin'."

"Sometimes I have bad dreams," said Jan.

"Mmmmmme, too," said Joseph.

"What happened to the baby?" asked Jan.

"By some stroke of luck, Frank's grandma reached the end of the fourth wall with the baby. Quick as a flash, he grabbed the both of them."

"That sure was a good thing," offered Jan, much relieved.

The storm seemed to be subsiding so Granny said, "Now that you know that Uncle Frank's grandma got safely back to her room with the baby, you boys can find your way to your beds to have a good sleep. I'll tell you more of my stories some other time."

177

The Birthday Surprise

Jan always remembered his little brother's birthday because it was two days before the Feast of Nativity of Mary.

"What is all that writing on your shirt?" asked Granny of Jan.

"You see," he explained, "Aunt Berti told me Mr. Dvořák wrote little music notes on his shirt cuffs. I guess he was making up a new song."

"That may be true," said Granny, "but he is an important musician and you are just a little boy, though a very good one, most of the time."

Jan wanted to give his small brother a special birthday present. He had to remind himself to pick some wild blackberries during the early birthday morning. He knew that Granny was making something for Joseph because every evening after they were supposed to be in bed, he had seen her plying her needle in front of the kitchen stove. What could she be making?

The day for celebrating rolled around, and Jan could see and smell the tasty liver dumplings and lambs' quarters that Aunt Berti was preparing for the occasion. He had helped gather the tiger lily blossoms as Granny made delicious salad with the petals.

"Goulash soup," called Aunt Berti to Uncle Frank, Granny, and the boys. "Joseph, you kin sit right close to yer grandma and brudder, Jan."

Joseph was all scrubbed for his birthday dinner. He was now six years old and a grown-up boy. Granny smiled at him.

"You can bring your stool closer to the table," said Granny.

What is on the seat? thought Joseph. It was the most mysterious-looking package, all wrapped in Calmar newspapers.

"Can you guess?" queried Granny. "I'll bet Jan can't."

"I know Granny made it. That's all I know," said Jan.

"You'll see what it is after we have our prayers."

All during the blessing, little Joseph wondered what was under those newspapers.

"Th—th—thank you all—lll for the pr—esents," said little Joseph.

Jan had helped Uncle Frank fire a brick with Joseph's name on it. Aunt Berti had knitted Joseph a nice warm scarf for the cold winters. But Granny's present was so mysterious, something very special under that old newspaper.

"I—I—w—w—want to se—e—e wh—what it is," said little Joseph.

Granny insisted that they first enjoy the dinner especially cooked by Aunt Berti. After they had eaten the poppy seed cake, topped with blackberries, Granny said, "Now you can look under the newspapers, Joseph."

Slowly the birthday boy lifted each page. What would he find on the bottom? What could it be? Something soft decorated with bits of bright-colored cottons, a patchwork of reds, greens, yellows, and blues. When Joseph lifted the object to see it more clearly, little bells started to jangle. There were three of them sewn onto the crown of a pointed cap.

"You can put it on," said Granny. "It's a clown hat. I made it different from other clown hats, but the Czech clowns always liked to wear hats. We loved them in the old country."

"C—c—can I b—b—be a clown?" asked Joseph.

"You will be a wonderful clown, the best one in Winneshiek County," said Granny.

At the Circus

The Winneshiek County Fair was over. Aunt Berti had won the prize for the best watermelon pickles. Granny displayed her latest quilt, which she was keeping for the family. The boys helped Uncle Frank at the shooting gallery by presenting the awards.

The greatest excitement of late summer had to do with the Hagenbeck Circus, which pitched its tent on the outskirts of Decorah toward Spillville. Uncle Frank drove a buggy full of children for the great event. There was Jan, Joseph, and two neighbors, James and Mareka.

Joseph wore the clown cap that Granny had given him. He was very excited at the circus parade when he saw a clown riding on a donkey.

"Can we get out of the buggy to see better?" asked Jan.

"Watch what yer doin' there," said Uncle Frank. "I'll rest the horses while you git yerselves t' that boardwalk over there."

Out they jumped, the four children, Joseph with his clown hat. Jan took Joseph's hand and pushed his way through the crowd. The other two children followed.

"Let's go toward the big tent to get some good seats," said James, aged eleven. "I have the tickets for all of us."

Jan motioned to Uncle Frank where they were going. Following James, the children kept one eye on the parade. While the brass band played "Stars and Stripes Forever," the costumed artists on mounted horses passed by. There was a cage with fancy gold-and-crimson pictures, and inside the cage was a real lion. Then a beautiful lady in a green-satin costume rode by on her black horse. Other riders in costumes followed while the calliope blared out familiar tunes.

Jan said to James, the oldest, "Uncle Frank said to wait inside close to the entrance of the tent."

"I think he said to go inside to find our seats," said James.

The children climbed up the rickety planks, which acted as temporary seats for the audience.

"Look at that clown over there across the ring," said Jan to Joseph. "He's talking to the ringmaster."

"I—l—l—love clowns," said little Joseph.

The children saw acrobats performing on horseback, some jumping from horse to horse. In a smaller circle was a human pyramid, all the performers riding on horses. Lady riders leaped over bright banners and through colored hoops. One acrobat with one foot on the saddle and one on the horse's head fired a shot at a distant target.

After a while Jan looked around for Uncle Frank. There he was, finally, pushing his way toward the area where the children sat. In his hands were some pink cotton cones, all sugary and beautiful. He had two in each hand. When he reached the children's seats, he said, "Sorry t'be late."

Then he handed out cotton cones.

"But where's m' little Joseph? Don't see him any-wheres."

"He was here just a minute ago," said Jan. "At least I thought he was right here."

"Well, he ain't here now. What could-a happened t' the little fella?"

Jan was worried. They all left their seats and pushed their way toward the entrance of the tent. They asked everybody if they had seen a little blond-haired boy with curly hair.

"All little kids have blond curly hair," said one father. "What was the boy wearing?"

"Has on a plaid shirt with suspenders. He has a clown hat on," added Jan.

"Ain't seen nobody like that."

Uncle Frank, Jan, and the two friends rushed out of the tent. Outside, beyond the entrance, were several side shows. There was a fat lady in one booth, another lady with four arms, and a snake charmer who was inviting the audience to come in her tent to see the captive snakes from the jungle. The painted lady said she had seen a little boy following one of the clowns.

"Which way, lady?" asked Uncle Frank.

"Nice kid," said the lady, "said he could sing. The clown asked him if he'd like to join Hagenbeck's Circus." She laughed.

"He can sing, all right," said Uncle Frank, getting more and more worried.

Jan was even more worried. He should have watched out for his young brother.

"Better all stick together," said Uncle Frank. "Maybe someone else could get lost."

"Let's go inside the tent again," urged Jan. "I bet Joseph is there somewhere."

They climbed back to their seats and looked out at the ring. It was just time for another clown act.

Yes, they could hardly believe their eyes, but a clown dressed in a patchwork costume of many colors was pulling a little red wagon with a little boy inside. The sign on the wagon said: LITTLE BOY LOST. The clown and the little boy were singing together.

"That's a Czech song!" shouted Jan. "The clown is from the old country, and he and Joseph are singing together!"

"Wait till Granny hears this story," said Uncle Frank. "She'll have another tale t'tell."

Now that little Joseph was found, the clown was happy to meet all of Joseph's family and friends. He said Joseph would make a good clown some day. He was happy he had such a nice family.

The Concert

At the end of the summer, the people of Spillville and Calmar, both young and old, attended a concert, the guest of honor being Antonín Dvořák, the famous musician from Czechoslovakia. A string quintet, composed in Spillville, was featured, Mr. Dvořák playing the first violin.

The concert opened with the chorus from *The Bartered Bride* of Smetana. After that a portion of Mozart's Mass was sung, Dvořák's friend playing the organ.

A children's chorus rendered a Czech folk song. Little Joseph was allowed to sing a few bars all by himself. Everyone was pleased, especially the good-natured Dvořák, who, during his short stay in Spillville, had won the hearts of the county folks. He was interested in the little boy who could sing but could not speak coherently.

On the last day of Dvořák's visit, the composer walked along the shores of the Turkey River. Perhaps he was deliberating on the talent of the Czech-American children. He was listening the last time to the birds of the fields and meadows, birds whose song he would not hear in his beloved Czechoslovakia. There was, especially the scarlet tanager whose song he imitated in his string quartet. He was grateful for America, his Czech compatriots, and the conservatory of music in New York that had invited him to come to this country. It would not be many days before his wife and six children would be settling down in their European homeland. The Negro melodies in his *New World Symphony* would open his heart to the American people, both black and white.

As for the two brothers, Jan and Joseph, they continued to circumvent the farm belonging to the ugly man. They sang in the children's chorus of Spillville and Calmar and learned to take care of all the animals on Granny's farm. In the evenings, sometimes by the kitchen stove, Granny would tell them tales of old Czechoslovakia (the country of the Czechs and the Slovaks). She told them how Jan Hus had led the people to liberty in 1415 and how the Czechs have always fought for liberty. This made the children very proud.

SAILOR'S SONG

Czech Folk Song

Brightly

1. Yo ho, heave ho! Pull my lads mer - ri - ly!
2. Yo ho, heave ho! Pull my lads cheer - i - ly!

Yo ho, heave ho! Yo ho, heave ho!
Yo ho, heave ho! Yo ho, heave ho!

Blow wind, blow loud and free! Blue waits the o - pen sea.
Good friends, fare - well to you! Long shall our hearts be true.

Yo ho, heave ho! Yo ho, heave ho!
Yo ho heave ho! Yo ho, heave ho!

FOLK DANCERS

Antonin Dvořák
(in *Slavic Dances*)

HUNTING SONG

A. Dvořák
From "Slavonic Dances."

Lively

1. Up, my lads, and join with me,
2. Keen of eye and sharp of ear,

The hunt - er's praise to tell;
He roams the for - est free,

Dai - ly bread, good luck, and health he wins,
With the wind and rain, or win - ter snows,

And finds re - nown as well.
No thought of care knows he.

Scarce the morn - ing's ear - ly beam
Home - ward with the set - ting sun,

Dyes the drow - sy hill - top red,
Light of step, he takes his way,

He must out to heed the call, Ere
Proud - ly bears his no - ble spoil To

yet the dews are shed.
greet the close of day.